Robert Browning

Lyrical and Dramatic Poems

Selected From the Works of Robert Browning

Robert Browning

Lyrical and Dramatic Poems
Selected From the Works of Robert Browning

ISBN/EAN: 9783744787819

Printed in Europe, USA, Canada, Australia, Japan

Cover: Foto ©Andreas Hilbeck / pixelio.de

More available books at **www.hansebooks.com**

BROWNING, ROBERT. LYRICAL AND DRAMATIC POEMS. Selected from the works of ROBERT BROWNING. With an extract from Stedman's "Victorian Poets." Edited by Edward T. Mason. New York: Henry Holt & Co., 1883. 12mo., pp. xviii, 275.

LYRICAL AND DRAMATIC POEMS. Selected from the works of ROBERT BROWNING. With an extract from Stedman's "Victorian Poets." Edited by Edward T. Mason. New York: Henry Holt & Co., 1883. 12mo, pp. xviii, 275.

POETRY. LYRICAL AND DRAMATIC POEMS. Selected from the works of ROBERT BROWNING. With an extract from Stedman's "Victorian Poets." Edited by Edward T. Mason. New York: Henry Holt & Co., 1883. 12mo, pp. xviii, 275.

LYRICAL AND
DRAMATIC POEMS

SELECTED FROM THE WORKS OF

ROBERT BROWNING

WITH AN EXTRACT FROM STEDMAN'S "VICTORIAN POETS."

EDITED BY

EDWARD T. MASON

NEW YORK
HENRY HOLT AND COMPANY
1883

CONTENTS.

	PAGE
PREFACE	V
AN EXTRACT FROM E. C. STEDMAN'S "VICTORIAN POETS".	I
CAVALIER TUNES:—MARCHING ALONG: GIVE A ROUSE: BOOT AND SADDLE	78
"HOW THEY BROUGHT THE GOOD NEWS FROM GHENT TO AIX " . . . . . , . . .	83
MULEYKEH	88
INCIDENT OF THE FRENCH CAMP	100
HERVE RIEL	103
HALBERT AND HOB	112
MARTIN RELPH	119
THE LOST LEADER	135
THE PIED PIPER OF HAMELIN	137
HOLY-CROSS DAY	153
SOLILOQUY OF THE SPANISH CLOISTER	161
THE LABORATORY.	165
A FORGIVENESS	169

Contents.

	PAGE
MEETING AT NIGHT.—PARTING AT MORNING	190
THE ITALIAN IN ENGLAND	192
UP AT A VILLA—DOWN IN THE CITY	200
THE ENGLISHMAN IN ITALY	207
HOME-THOUGHTS FROM ABROAD	221
THE GUARDIAN ANGEL	223
SONG	227
EVELYN HOPE	228
ABT VOGLER	232
SAUL	242
PROSPICE	274

PREFACE.

The object of this book is to excite a wider interest in the works of Robert Browning. Its contents have been selected with special reference to the large number of readers who can enjoy those portions of his poetry which are clear and melodious, and do not enjoy those which tax the ingenuity and fail to please the ear.

The fame of this poet is world-wide. He has inspired enthusiastic devotion in minds of the highest order; yet he is little read. Why is this? The fault is in the poet: not in the public. Let us first take a fair view of the ugly side of this subject. It must be confessed that Browning often fails to make himself understood, and that, where his meaning is plain, it is often expressed in harsh and jagged lines. One cause of his obscurity is his fondness for out-of-the-way themes, which he treats with entire indifference to the fact that they are not so familiar to his readers as to himself ; another cause is the peculiarity of his style ; his habit of contraction, and his use of idiomatic forms hitherto unknown to the English language. His devotees have excused — even justified and commended — his obscurity, and their loyalty has sometimes betrayed them into utterances which come dangerously near being nonsense. It has been said that he cares so much for the spirit of his work, that he is quite regardless of its form ; that he has such reverence for his thought that he chooses to present it in its naked simplicity. The essential fallacy of such criticism is, that it ignores the fact that poetry is always dependent upon form, that the excellence of verse depends upon perfection of structure. It is needless to enlarge upon so elementary a principle of the poetic art. Mr. Nettleship, in the course of an essay upon *Sordello*, published in 1868, says : —

"It seems to me that we may find good reasons for the existence of these defects, so-called. He evidently considers that his first duty as a poet is to give us direct from the fountain-head, either his perceptions, so far as they can be expressed in language, or his thoughts : that his toil should be spent in digging out straight from its hiding-place the pure unalloyed perception or thought for men to see. Thus his argument would be, either that so long as the true worth of the metal is seen, any labor spent in improving or making smooth its actual visible shape is a waste of power, or that such labor if bestowed has only the effect of lessening the bulk and tarnishing the brilliancy of the untouched conception. " In view of the facts of the case, ordinary, uninspired common sense revolts against this. What if the mass quarried out comes "in such a questionable shape"— is so chaotic and mysterious, that men not only doubt if it be gold, but cannot even decide whether it be mineral, animal, or vegetable? Fitz Hugh Ludlow, one of the most genial and acute of critics, one, too, who loved to "pluck

out the heart of a mystery," himself a warm ad-
mirer of Browning — once said of this same *Sordello*,
—" He might as well have shuffled the words together in a hat, and tumbled them out, pell mell,
upon the table. " There is an old story, in the
same connection, which is so good and suggestive
that it will bear re-telling. Douglas Jerrold, was
recovering from a severe illness ; while he was still
confined to his bed, *Sordello*, then newly published,
was brought to him. In a few moments he called
eagerly to his wife, who came from an adjoining
room, and found the invalid sitting upright in bed,
with an expression of grave anxiety and apprehen-
sion upon his face. " Take this ! read that page !"
She obeyed, Jerrold watching her the while with
intense earnestness. "Well? well?" he exclaimed,
when she looked up from the volume, " Do you
understand it ?—Does it convey any idea to your
mind?" "No, indeed ! Not the slightest ! " "Thank
God !" said Jerrold, sinking back upon his pillow,
"Thank God! I thought I had lost my reasoning
powers ! "

Present to any chance company of twenty fairly well educated people, such lines as these : —

> "O call him not culprit, this Pontiff !
> Be hard on this Kaiser ye won't if
> Ye take into con-si-de ration
> What dangers attend elevation !" —

or these : —

> "They turned on him.   Dumb menace in that mouth,
> Malice in that unstridulosity !
> He cannot but intend some stroke of state
> Shall signalize his passage into peace
> Out of the creaking ; hinder transference
> O' the Hohenstielers – Schwanganese to King,
> Pope, autocrat, or socialist republic ! That's
> Exact the cause his lips unlocked would cry."

— Can there be any doubt what the general verdict would be ? If poetry is indeed an art, and if the office of that art is to present worthy themes in an especially clear and attractive manner — how shall we find excuse for such work as this ?

The reader may think that all this is foreign to my purpose, and it does seem an odd way to recommend an author ; yet, uncourteous and uncalled-for as these observations may appear, in the present instance there are good reasons for them. Profoundly impressed by the greatness of Browning's genius, recognizing his rare qualities, believing him to be in some respects the greatest poet of his age — I am yet convinced that no attempt to show his claims to popular regard can be consistent or successful, which does not proceed upon a frank admission of his many and glaring faults. Some of his admirers have labored to prove him great in virtue of his defects ; may it not be wiser to show that he is great in spite of those defects? Let us try to see, then, why it is that this poet, from whom the majority of intelligent readers turn away, despairing, if not disgusted, is hailed as master by some singers of well assured fame, and is applauded by critics whose judgment commands respect.

He is a master of the technicalities of his art, and is endowed with a genuine gift of song. Few poets have held so easy and so assured a mastery over many and widely varied rhythmical forms. The prevailing tendency of his verse is toward vigor rather than beauty ; yet he has written lines which place him in the foremost rank of rhythmical melodists ; lines filled with the spirit of music, gracious, serenely beautiful, challenging comparison with the verse of Spenser or of Keats : —

"And I first played the tune all our sheep know, as, one
  after one,
So docile they come to the pen door, till folding be done.
They are white and untorn by the bushes, for lo, they have fed
Where the long grasses stifle the water within the stream's bed ;
And now one after one seeks its lodging, as star follows star
Into eve and the blue far above us — so blue and so far !"—

Lines such as these will linger in the memory for many a year ! Some of his poems are lyrical in the strictest sense, suggesting, claiming the accompaniment of song — and well fitted to be sung. For instance, nothing could be better in their way than the *Cavalier Tunes*, especially the first, *Marching Along*. This is a true song. Silks rustle, plumes wave, swords flash, as the gallants start from their carouse ; we hear the rollicking voices of the madcap band as they lustily troll out their defiant battle-song, and we would fain join in the ringing chorus.

He is eminently successful in narrative poetry, and knows thoroughly well how to tell a story, be it grave or gay. He can seize the essential features of a great action or a strange experience, and, with a few bold strokes, present a picture all aglow with color and instinct with life, leaving on the mind an impression bright as a diamond. Who can ever forget the wild gallop from Ghent to Aix, or that heroic boy who fell dead at Napoleon's feet — the smile upon his lips? On the other hand, he can take some odd legend, like that of the *Pied Piper*, and sustain our interest in it through page after page; wandering on from sheer love of story-telling, adding fresh incidents, inventing new surprises, weaving in quaint details, while we follow him as eagerly as ever the children of Hamelin ran after the fascinating piper. Humor forms a prominent element in his work; and the quality of his humor is very remarkable, both for its strength and variety; his range extends from easy pleasantry and good-natured banter, to grotesqueness as grim as Holbein's Dance of Death.

He does not often give us descriptions of nature, but scattered throughout his works there are passages which show that he is not insensible to nature's charm ; passages of simple and quiet loveliness, which sink deep into the heart, without bewildering the brain. Such are to be found in *Saul*, and in the picturesquely descriptive *Englishman in Italy ;* but the finest example of his power to portray nature, is the exquisite lyric, *Home-thoughts from Abroad ;* here there is absolutely no suggestion of the " smell of the lamp " ; all is fresh and bright and sweet — the very breath of an English spring-time caught, and stored away for us in a book ! Having thus glanced at some aspects of his verse which invite comparison with the work of other men, we may consider the poet's peculiar and characteristic excellence.

Human nature is the theme and inspiration of the greater portion of Browning's poetry Always a close observer and a keen analyst, in this field of study his observation becomes most close, his analysis most searching and subtle. Human nature attracts and absorbs him beyond all else, leading him to scan with eager eyes alike the past and the present, to mingle with men of every race and every station Perhaps the difficulty of his task may suggest some explanation of his frequent obscurity. The primary object of his work is the portrayal of character ; he would show what men are, not what they do ; incident and action are valued by him only in so far as they illustrate the inner life. To this end he subordinates everything, all the fruits of his scholarship, all the resources of his art, and in the pursuit of this object he has achieved his highest success, and made for himself a unique place among the poets of the world.

It is his highest praise, that while his chief study is humanity, the revelation of man's " heart of heart, " his song is cheerful and inspiring, declaring hopes, not fears, certainties, not doubts ; passing by apparent failure in the present, to dwell upon final success. In an age of negation and querulous doubt, negation finds but little room in Browning's philosophy — pessimism, none. He is a poet of active faith, and, therefore, of strength and comfort. He utters no wail over the destiny of mankind. Though he clearly recognizes the existence of " the heartache, and the thousand natural shocks that flesh is heir to ; " though he sees pain and sorrow with widely and deeply sympathetic vision, he is yet able to look forward toward the consummation of all things, with a serene assurance of ultimate triumph for the race. This spirit constantly manifests itself in his work ; it animates the dreamily tender sentiment of *Evelyn Hope*, it may be traced more clearly in the passionate cry of *Abt Vogler*, and it rises to still nobler heights in *Prospice*, and in the rapt ecstasy of the shepherd-boy, the inspired bard and seer, who proclaims deliverance to Saul.

With two exceptions — *Abt Vogler* and *Saul* — no poem in this volume can be for a moment regarded as obscure. The aim has been to show the poet at his best ; but the principle of selection has made it necessary to exclude many poems of rare beauty and excellence. No extracts have been made from the longer poems, although they contain much that is clear and admirable ; such fragments can seldom produce a satisfactory impression, or do any justice to their author.   Despite their occasional obscurity, it was found impossible to exclude *Abt Vogler* and *Saul,* for both of these poems are among the best illustrations of the optimism which is so important an element of Browning's genius ; and, among his shorter poems, Saul is, perhaps, the one which most conspicuously manifests that creative imagination, which is the highest faculty that a poet can possess.

I am indebted to Messrs. Houghton, Mifflin, & Co. for permission to make use of the ninth chapter of Mr. Stedman's *Victorian Poets,* which is here re-printed. This is an especially valuable introduction to the study of Browning ; being a comprehensive and judicial estimate of the poet's merits and de-merits, by a not unfriendly critic.

ROBERT BROWNING.*

In a study of Browning, the most original and unequal of living poets, three features obviously present themselves. His dramatic gift, so rare in these times, calls for recognition and analysis ; his method — the eccentric quality of his expression — constantly intrudes upon the reader ; lastly, the moral of his verse warrants a closer examination than we give to the sentiments of a more conventional poet My own perception of the spirit which his poetry, despite his assumption of a purely dramatic purpose, has breathed from the outset, is one which I shall endeavor to convey in simple and direct terms.

Various other examples have served to illustrate the phases of a poet's life, but Browning arouses

---

* Reprinted from E. C. Stedman's *Victorian Poets*, by permission of Messrs. Houghton, Mifflin, & Co.

discussion with respect to the elements of poetry as an art. Hitherto I have given some account of an author's career and writings before proffering a critical estimate of the latter. But this man's genius is so peculiar, and he has been so isolated in style and purpose, that I know not how to speak of his works without first seeking a key to their interpretation, and hence must partially reverse the order hitherto pursued.

I.

It is customary to call Browning a dramatist, and without doubt he represents the dramatic element, such as it is, of the recent English school. He counts among his admirers many intellectual persons, some of whom pronounce him the greatest dramatic poet since Shakespeare, and one has said that " it is to him we must pay homage for whatever is good, and great, and profound, in the second period of the Poetic Drama of England."

This may be true ; nevertheless, it also should be declared, with certain modifications, that Robert

Browning, in the original sense of the term, is not a dramatic poet at all.

Procter, in the preface to a collection of his own songs, remarks with precision and truth : " It is, in fact, this power of forgetting himself, and of imagining and fashioning characters different from his own, which constitutes the dramatic quality. A man who can set aside his own idiosyncrasy is half a dramatist." Although Browning's earlier poems were in the form of plays, and have a dramatic purpose, they are at the opposite remove, in spirit and method, from the models of the true histrionic era, — the work of Fletcher, Webster, and Shakespeare. They have the sacred rage and fire, but the flame is that of Browning, and not of the separate creations which he strives to inform.

The early drama was the mouthpiece of a passionate and adventurous era. The stage bore to the period the relations of the modern novel and newspaper to our own, not only holding the mirror up to nature, but showing the " very age and body of the time." It was a vital growth, sprung from the people, and having a reflex action upon their imagination and conduct. Even in Queen Anne's day the theatre was the meeting-place of wits, and, if the plays were meaner, it was because they copied the manners of an artificial world. But, in either case, the playwrights were in no more hazard of representing their own natures, in one rôle after another, than are the leader-writers in their versatile articles upon topics of our day. They invented a score of characters, or took them from real life, grouped them with consummate effect, placed them in dramatic situations, lightened tragedy with mirth, mellowed comedy with pathos, and produced a healthful and objective dramatic literature. They looked outward, not inward : their imagination was the richer for it, and of a more varied kind.

The stage still has its office, but one more subsidiary than of old. Our own age is no less stirring than was the true dramatic period, and is far more subtile in thought. But the poets fail to represent it objectively, and the drama does not act as a safety-valve for the escape of surplus passion and desire. That office the novelists have undertaken, while the press brings its dramas to every fireside. Yet the form of the play still seems to a poet the most comprehensive mould in which to cast a masterpiece. It is a combination of scenic and plastic art ; it includes monologue, dialogue, and song,— action and meditation,— man and woman, the lover, the soldier, and the thinker,— all vivified by the imagination, and each essential to the completeness of the whole. Even to poets like Byron, who have no perception of natures differing from their own, it has a fascination as a vehicle of expression, and the result is seen in "Sardanapalus" and "Cain." Hence the closet-drama ; and although praiseworthy efforts, as in " Virginius" and "Ion," have been made to revive the early method, these modern stage-plays often are unpoetical and tame. Most of what is excellent in our dramatic verse is to be found in plays that could not be successfully enacted.

While Browning's earlier poems are in the dramatic form, his own personality is manifest in the speech and movement of almost every character of each piece. His spirit is infused, as if by metempsychosis, within them all, and forces each to assume a strange Pentecostal tone, which we discover to be that of the poet himself. Bass, treble, or recitative,— whether in pleading, invective, or banter,— the voice still is there. But while his characters have a common manner and diction, we become so wonted to the latter that it seems like a new dialect which we have mastered for the sake of its literature. This feeling is acquired after some acquaintance with his poems, and not upon a first or casual reading of them.

The brief, separate pieces, which he terms "dramatic lyrics," are just as properly dramas as are many of his five-act plays. Several of the latter were intended for stage-production. In these we feel that the author's special genius is hampered, so that the student of Browning deems them less rich and rare than his strictly characteristic essays. Even in the most conventional, this poet cannot refrain from the long monologues, stilted action, and metaphysical discursion, which mark the closet-drama and unfit a composition for the stage. His chief success is in the portrayal of single characters and specific moods.

I would not be understood to praise his originality at the expense of his greatness. His mission has been that of exploring those secret regions which generate the forces whose outward phenomena it is for the playwrights to illustrate. He has opened a new field for the display of emotional power,— founding, so to speak, a sub-dramatic school of poetry whose office is to follow the workings of the mind, to discover the impalpable elements of which human motives and passions are composed. The greatest forces are the most elusive, the unseen mightier than the seen ; modern genius chooses to seek for the under-currents of the soul rather than to depict acts and situations. Browning, as the poet of pyschology, escapes to that stronghold whither, as I have said, science and materialism are not yet prepared to follow him. How shall the chemist read the soul ? No former poet has so relied upon this province for the excursions of his muse. True, he explores by night, stumbles, halts, has vague ideas of the topography, and often goes back upon his course. But, though others complete the unfinished work of Columbus, it is to him that we award the glory of discovery,— not to the engineers and colonists that succeed him, however firmly they plant themselves and correctly map out the now undisputed land.

II.

Browning's manner is so eccentric as to challenge attention and greatly affect our estimate of him as a poet. Eccentricity is not a proof of genius, and even an artist should remember that originality consists not only in doing things differently, but also in "doing things better." The genius of Shakespeare and Molière enlarged and beautified their style; it did not distort it. Again, the grammarian's statement is true, that Poetry is a means of Expression. A poet may differ from other men in having profounder emotions and clearer perceptions, but this is not for him to assume, nor a claim which they are swift to grant. The lines,

> "O many are the poets that are sown
>   By Nature ! men endowed with highest gifts,
>   The vision and the faculty divine ;
>   Yet wanting the accomplishment of verse,"

imply that the recognized poet is one who gives voice, in expressive language, to the common thought and feeling which lie deeper than ordinary speech. He is the interpreter : moreover, he is the maker,— an artist of the beautiful, the inventor of harmonious numbers which shall be a lure and a repose.

A poet, however emotional or rich in thought, must not fail to express his conception and make his work attractive. Over-possession is worth less than a more commonplace faculty ; he that has the former is a sorrow to himself and a vexation to his hearers, while one whose speech is equal to his needs, and who knows his limitations, adds something to the treasury of song, and is able to shine in

his place, "and be content.' Certain effects are
suggested by nature; the poet discovers new com-
binations within the ground which these afford.
Ruskin has shown that in the course of years, though
long at fault, the masses come to appreciate any
admirable work. By inversion, if, after a long time
has passed, the world still is repelled by a singer,
and finds neither rest nor music in him, the fault is
not with the world ; there is something deficient in
his genius,— he is so much the less a poet.

The distinction between poetry and prose must
be sharply observed. Poetry is an art,— a specific
fact, which, owing to the vagueness fostered by
minor wits, we do not sufficiently insist upon. We
hear it said that an eloquent prose passage is poetry,
that a sunset is a poem, and so on. This is well
enough for rhetorical effect yet wholly untrue, and
no poet should permit himself to talk in that way.
Poetry is poetry, because it differs from prose ; it is
artificial, and gives us pleasure because we know it
to be so. It is beautiful thought expressed in rhythmical form, not half expressed or uttered in the

form of prose. It is a metrical structure; a spirit
not disembodied, but in the flesh,— so as to affect
the senses of living men. Such is the poetry of
Earth ; what that of a more spiritual region may be
I know not. Milton and Keats never were in doubt
as to the meaning of the art. It is true that fine
prose is a higher form of expression than wretched
verse ; but when a distinguished young English poet
thus writes to me,—

"My own impression is that Verse is an inferior, or infant,
form of speech, which will ultimately perish altogether. . .
The Seer, the Vates, the teacher of a new truth, is single,
while what you call artists are legion,"

— when I read these words, I remember that the
few great seers have furnished models for the simplest and greatest form of art ; I feel that this poet
is growing heretical with respect, not to the law of
custom, but to a law which is above us all ; I fear
to discover a want of beauty, a vague transcendentalism, rather than a clear inspiration, in his verse,
—to see him become prosaic and substitute rhetoric
for passion, realism for naturalness, affectation for

lofty thought, and, "having been praised for bluntness," to "affect a saucy roughness." In short, he is on the edge of danger. Yet his remark denotes a just impatience of forms so hackneyed that, once beautiful, they now are stale and corrupt. It may be necessary, with the Pre-Raphaelites, to escape their thraldom and begin anew. But the poet is a creator, not an iconoclast, and never will tamely endeavor to say in prose what can only be expressed in song. And I have faith that my friend's wings will unfold, in spite of himself, and lift him bravely as ever on their accustomed flights.

Has the lapse of years made Browning any more attractive to the masses, or even to the judicious few? He is said to have "succeeded by a series of failures," and so he has, as far as notoriety means success, and despite the recent increase of his faults. But what is the fact which strikes the admiring and sympathetic student of his poetry and career? Distrusting my own judgment, I asked a clear and impartial thinker,— "How does Browning's work impress you?" His reply, after a moment's consider-

ation was: " Now that I try to formulate the sen-
sation which it always has given me, his work seems
that of a grand intellect painfully striving for ade-
quate use and expression, and never quite attain-
ing either." This was, and is, precisely my own
feeling. The question arises, What is at fault ?
Browning's genius, his chosen mode of expression,
his period, or one and all of these ? After the
flush of youth is over, a poet must have a wise
method, if he would move ahead. He must improve
upon instinct by experience and common-sense.
There is something amiss in one who has to grope
for his theme and cannot adjust himself to his period ; especially in one who cannot agreeably handle
such themes as he arrives at. More than this, however, is the difficulty in Browning's case. Expression is the flower of thought ; a fine imagination is
wont to be rhythmical and creative, and many passages, scattered throughout Browning's works, show
that his is no exception. It is a certain caprice
or perverseness of method, that, by long practice,
has injured his gift of expression ; while an abnor-

mal power of ratiocination, and a prosaic regard for details, have handicapped him from the beginning. Besides, in mental arrogance and scorn of authority, he has insulted Beauty herself, and furnished too much excuse for small offenders. What may be condoned in one of his breed is intolerable when mimicked by every jackanapes and self-appointed reformer.

A group of evils, then, has interfered with the greatness of his poetry. His style is that of a man caught in a morass of ideas through which he has to travel,— wearily floundering, grasping here and there, and often sinking deeper until there seems no prospect of getting through. His latest works have been more involved and excursive, less beautiful and elevating, than most of those which preceded them. Possibly his theory is that which was his wife's instinct,— a man being more apt than a woman with some reason for what he does,— that poetry is valuable *only* for the statement which it makes, and must always be subordinate thereto. Nevertheless, Emerson, in this country, seems to have followed a kindred method ; and who of our poets is greater, or so wise ?

III.

Browning's early lyrics, and occasional passages of recent date, show that he has melodious intervals, and can be very artistic with no loss of original power. Often the ring of his verse is sonorous, and overcomes the jagged consonantal diction with stirring lyrical effect. The "Cavalier Tunes" are examples. Such choruses as

> "Marching along, fifty-score strong,
>   Great-hearted gentlemen, singing this song !"

> "King Charles, and who'll do him right now ?
>   King Charles, and who's ripe for fight now ?
>   Give a rouse : here's, in Hel!'s despite now,
>   King Charles !"

— these, with, "Boot, saddle, to horse, and away !" show that Browning can put in verse the spirit of a historic period, and has, or had, in him the making of a lyric poet. How fresh and wholesome this work ! Finer still that superb stirrup-piece, best of

its class in the language, "How they brought the
good news from Ghent to Aix." "Ratisbon" and
"The Lost Leader," no less, are poems that fasten
themselves upon literature, and will not be forgotten.
The old fire flashes out, thirty years after, in
"Hervé Riel," another vigorous production,—
unevenly sustained, but on a level with Longfellow's
legendary ballads and sagas.   From among lighter
pieces I will select for present mention two, very
unlike each other ; one, as delightful a child's poem
as ever was written, in fancy and airy extravagance,
and having a wildness and pathos all its own,— the
daintest bit of folk-lore in English verse,— to what
should I refer but "The Pied Piper of Hamelin ?"
The author made a strong bid for the love of children, when he placed "By Robert Browning" at its
head, in the collection of his poems.   The other,

> "Beautiful Evelyn Hope is dead !
>   Sit and watch by her side an hour,"

appeals, like Wordsworth's "She dwelt among the
untrodden ways," and Landor's "Rose Aylmer," to

the hearts of learned and unlettered, one and all.

Browning's style is the more aggressive, because, in compelling beauty itself to suffer a change and conform to all exigencies, it presents such a contrast to the refined art of our day. I have shown that much of this is due to natural awkwardness,— but that the author is able, on fortunate occasions, to better his work, has just been amply illustrated. More often he either has let his verse have its way, or has shaped a theory of art by his own restrictions, and with that contempt for the structure of his song which Plato and St. Paul entertained for their fleshly bodies. If the mischief ceased here, it would not be so bad, but his genius has won pupils who copy his vices without his strength. He and his wife injured each the other's style as much as they sustained their common aspiration and love of poesy. To be sure, there was a strange similarity, by nature, between their modes of speech; and what I have said of the woman's obscurity, affectations, elisions, will apply to the man's—with his

2

i'thes and *o'thes*, his dashes, breaks, halting measures, and oracular exclamations that convey no dramatic meaning to the reader. Her verse is the more spasmodic ; his, the more metaphysical, and, while effective in the best of his dramatic lyrics, is constantly running into impertinences worse than those of his poorest imitators, and which would not be tolerated for a moment in a lesser poet. Parodies on his style, thrown off as burlesques, are more intelligible than much of his " Dramatis Personæ." Unlike Tennyson, he does not comprehend the *limits* of a theme ; nor has he an idea of the *relative importance* either of themes or details ; his mind is so alert that its minutest turn of thought must be uttered ; he dwells with equal precision upon the meanest and grandest objects, and laboriously jots down every point that occurs to him,— parenthesis within parenthesis,— until we have a tangle as intricate as the line drawn by an anemometer upon the recording-sheet. The poem is all zigzag, crisscross, at odds and ends,— and, though we come out right at last, strength and patience are exhausted in

mastering it.   Apply the rule that nothing should be
told in verse which can be told in prose, and half
his measures would be condemned ; since their chief
metrical purpose is, through the stress of rhythm, to
fix our attention, by a certain unpleasant fascination, upon a process of reasoning from which it
otherwise would break away.

For so much of Browning's crudeness as comes
from inability to express himself, or to find a proper
theme, he may readily be forgiven ; but whatever is
due to real or assumed irreverence for the divine
art, among whose votaries he stands enrolled, is a
grievous wrong, unworthy of the humble and
delightful spirit of a true craftsman.   He forgets
that art is the bride of the imagination, from whose
embraces true creative work must spring.   Lastly,
concerning realism, while poets are, as Mrs. Browning said, "your only truth-tellers," it is not well that
repulsive or petty facts should always be recorded ;
only the high, essential truths demand a poet's
illumination.   The obscurity wherein Browning dis-
guises his realism is but the semblance of imagina-

tion,— a mist through which rugged details jut out, while the central truth is feebly to be seen.

IV.

After a period of study at the London University young Browning, in 1832, went to Italy, and acquired a remarkable knowledge of the Italian life and language. He mingled with all classes of the people, mastered details, and rummaged among the monasteries of Lombardy and Venice, studying mediæval history, and filling his mind with the relics of a bygone time. All this had much to do with the bent of his subsequent work, and possibly was of more benefit to his learning than to his ideality.

At the age of twenty-three he published his first drama, *Paracelsus*, a most unique production,— strictly speaking, a metaphysical dialogue, as noticeable for analytic power as the romances of Keats for pure beauty. It did not find many readers, but no man of letters could peruse it without seeing that a genuine poet had come to light. From that time the author moved in the literary society of London, and was recognized as one who had done something and might do something more. The play is " Faust," with the action and passion, and much of the poetry and music,— upon which the fascination of the German work depends,— omitted ; the hero resembles " Faust " in the double aspiration to know and to enjoy, to search out mystical knowledge, yet drink at all the fountains of pleasure,— lest, after a long struggle, failing of knowledge, he should have lived in vain. It must be understood that Mr. Browning's Paracelsus was his own creation : a man of heroic longings, observed at various intervals, from his twentieth year, in which he leaves his native hamlet until he dies at the age of forty-eight,— obscure, and with his ideal seemingly unattained ; not the juggler, empiric, and charlatan of history, whose record the poet frankly gives us in a footnote.

This poem has every characteristic of Browning's genius. The verse is as strong and as weak as the best and worst he has composed during thirty years, and is pitched in a key now familiar to us all.

" Paracelsus," the fruit of his youth, serves as well for a study of this poet as any later effort, and, though inferior to " Pippa Passes " and " In a Balcony," is much better than his newest romance in blank verse. I cannot agree with critics who say that he did his poorest work first and has been moving along an ascending scale ; on the contrary, his faults and beauties have been somewhat evenly distributed throughout his career. We are vexed in " Paracelsus " by a vice that haunts him still, — that tedious garrulity which, however relieved by beautiful passages, palls on the reader and weakens the general effect. As an offset, he displays in this poem, with respect to every kind of poetic faculty except the sense of proportion, gifts equal to those of any compeer. By turns he is surpassingly fine. We have strong dramatic diction : —

> " Festus, strange secrets are let out by Death,
> Who blabs so oft the follies of this world :
> And I am Death's familiar, as you know.
> I helped a man to die, some few weeks since ;
>
> .   .   .   .
>
>   .   .   .   .   No mean trick

> He left untried ; and truly wellnigh wormed
> All traces of God's finger out of him.
> Then died, grown old ; and just an hour before —
> Having lain long with blank and soulless eyes —
> He sate up suddenly, and with natural voice
> Said, that in spite of thick air and closed doors
> God told him it was June , and he knew well,
> Without such telling, harebells grew in June ;
> And all that kings could ever give or take
> Would not be precious as those blooms to him."

The conception is old as Shakespeare, but the manner is large and effective. Few authors vary the breaks and pauses of their blank verse so naturally as Browning, and none can so well dare to extend the proper limits of a poem. Here, as in later plays, he shows a more realistic perception of scenery and nature than is common with dramatic poets. We have a bit of painting at the outset, in the passage beginning,

> " Nay Autumn wins you best by this its mute
> Appeal to sympathy for its decay ! "

and others, equally fine and true, are scattered throughout the dialogue.

" Paracelsus " is meant to illustrate the growth
and progress of a lofty spirit, groping in the darkness of his time. He first aspires to knowledge,
and fails ; then to pleasure and knowledge, and
equally fails — to human eyes. The secret ever
seems close at hand : —

> "Ah, the curse, Aprile, Aprile !
> We get so near — so very, very near !
> 'Tis an old tale : Jove strikes the Titans down
> Not when they set about their mountain-piling,
> But when another rock would crown their work !"

Now, it is a part of Browning's life-long habit,
that he here refuses to judge by ordinary standards,
and makes the hero's attainment lie even in his failure and death. There are few more daring asser-
tions of the soul's absolute freedom than the words
of Festus, impressed by the nobility of his dying
friend : —

> " I am for noble Aureole, God !
> I am upon his side, come weal or woe !
> His portion shall be mine !   He has done well !
> I would have sinned, had I been strong enough,

As he has sinned !   Reward him, or I waive
Reward !   If thou canst find no place for him
He shall be king elsewhere, and I will be
His slave forever !   There are two of us !"

The drama is well worth preserving, and even now a curious and highly suggestive study.   Its lyrical interludes seem out of place.   As an author's first essay, it promised more for his future than if it had been a finished production, and in any other case but that of the capricious, tongue-tied Browning, the promise might have been abundantly fulfilled.

In "Strafford," his second drama, the interest also centres upon the struggles and motives of one heroic personage, this time entangled in a fatal mesh of great events.   Apparently the poet, after some experience of authorship, wished to commend his work to popular sympathy, and tried to write a play that should be fitted for the stage ; hence a tragedy dedicated to Macready, of which the chief character,— the hapless Earl of Strafford,— was assumed by that tragedian, but with no marked success. The action, in compliance with history, moves with sufficient rapidity, yet in a confused and turbulent way. The characters are eccentrically drawn, and are more serious and mystical than even the gloom of their period would demand. It is hard to perceive the motives of Lady Carlisle and the Queen ; there is no underplot of love in the play, to develop the womanly element, nor has it the humor of the great playwrights,— so essential to dramatic contrast, and for which the Puritans and the London populace might afford rich material. Imagine Macready stalking portentously through the piece, the audience trying to follow the story, and bored beyond endurance by the solemn speeches of Pym and Strafford, which answer for a death-scene at the close. The language is more natural than is usual with Browning, but here, where he is least eccentric, he becomes tame — until we see that he is out of his element, and prefer his striking psychology to a forced attempt at writing of the academic kind.

Something of this must have struck the poet himself for, as if chagrined at his failure, he swung back

to the other extreme, and beyond his early starting-
place ; farther, happily, than any point he since has
ventured to reach.   In no one of his recent works
has he been quite so "hard," loquacious, and im-
practicable as in the renowned nondescript entitled
Sordello.   Twenty-three years after its appearance
he owned that its "faults of expression were many,"
and added, "but with care for a man or book such
would be surmounted." The acknowledgment was
partial.   "Sordello " is a fault throughout, in conception and execution : nothing is "expressed, "
not even the "incidents in the development of a
soul," though such incidents may have had some
nebulous origin in the poet's mind. It is asking
too much of our care for a book or a man that we
should surmount this chaotic mass of word-building.
Carlyle's "Sartor Resartus" is a hard study, but,
once entered upon, how poetical ! what lofty
episodes ! what wisdom, beauty, and scorn ! Few
such treasures await him that would read the eleven
thousand verses into which the fatal facility of the
rhymed-heroic measure has led the muse of Brown-

ing.   The structure, by its very ugliness and bulk, like some half buried colossus in the desert, may survive a lapse of time.   I cannot persuade myself to solicit credit for deeper insight by differing from the common judgment with regard to this unattractive prodigy.

It had its uses, seemingly, in acting as a purge to cleanse the visual humors of the poet's eyes and to leave his general system in an auspicious condition. His next six years were devoted to the composition of a picturesque group of dramas,—the exact order of which escapes me, but which finally were collected in *Bells and Pomegranates*, a popular edition, issued in serial numbers, of this maturer work. "Luria," "King Victor and King Charles," and "The Return of the Druses," are stately pieces, historical or legendary, cast in full stage-form.   In Luria we again see Browning's favorite characterization, from a different point of view.   This is a large-moulded, suffering hero, akin, if disturbed in conscience, to Wallenstein,— if devoted and magnanimous, to Othello.   Luria, the Moor, is like

Othello in many ways: a brave and skillful general, who serves Florence (instead of Venice), and declares,

> "I can and have perhaps obliged the state,
>   Nor paid a mere son's duty."

He is so true and simple, that Domizia says of him,

> "How plainly is true greatness charactered
>   By such unconsciousness as Luria's here,
>   And sharing least the secret of itself!"

Browning makes devotion to an ideal or trust, however unworthy of it, the chief trait of this class of personages. Strafford dies in behalf of ungrateful Charles ; Luria is sacrificed by the Florence he has saved, and destroys himself at the moment when love and honor are hastening, too late, to crown him. Djabal, false to himself, is true to the cause of the Druses, and at last dies in expiation of his fault. Valence, in "Colombe's Birthday," shows devotion of a double kind, but is rewarded for his fidelity and honor. Luitolfo, in "A Soul's Tragedy," is of a kindred type. But I am anticipating. The language

of " Luria " often is in the grand manner. In depict-
ing the Moorish general and his friend Husain,—
brooding, generous children of the sun,— the
soldierly Tiburzio, painted with a few master-
strokes,— and in the element of Italian craft and
intrigue, the author is at home and well served by
his knowledge of mediæval times. That is an eloquent
speech of Domizia, near the end of the fourth act.
Despite the poverty of action, and the prolonged
harangues, this drama is worthy of its dedication to
Landor and the wish that it might be " read by his
light " : almost worthy (Landor always weighed out
gold for silver !) of the old bard"s munificent return
of praise : —

> " Shakespeare is not our poet but the world's,
> Therefore on him no speech ! and brief for thee,
> Browning ! Since Chaucer was alive and hale,
> No man hath walked along our roads with step
> So active, so inquiring eye, or tongue
> So varied in discourse.   But warmer climes
> Give brighter plumage, stronger wing : the breeze
> Of Alpine height thou playest with, borne on
> Beyond Sorrento and Amalfi, where
> The Siren waits thee, singing song for song."

'The Return of the Druses," with its scenic and choric effects, is like some of Byron's plays : the scene, an isle of the Sporades ; the legend, half Venetian, half Oriental, one that only Browning could make available. The girl Anael is an impassioned character, divided between adoration for Hakeem, the god of her race,— whom she believes incarnate in Djabal,— and her love for Djabal as a man. The tragedy, amid a good deal of trite and pedantic language, is marked by heroic situations and sudden dramatic catastrophes. Several brilliant points are made : one, where the Prefect lifts the arras, on the other side of which death awaits him, and says,—

> " This is the first time for long years I enter
> Thus, without feeling just as I lifted
> The lid up of my tomb !   .   .   .   .
>
> .   .   .   .   .
>
> Let me repeat — for the first time, no draught
> Coming as from a sepulchre salutes me ! "

A moment, and the dagger is through his heart. Another such is the wonder and contempt of Anael at finding Djabal no deity, but an impostor; while perhaps the most telling point in the whole series of Browning's plays is her cry of *Hakeem!* made when she comes to denounce Djabal, but, moved by love, proclaims him as the god, and falls dead with the effort. The poet, however, is justly censured for too frequently taking off his personages by the intensity of their own passions, without recourse to the dagger and bowl. He rarely does it after the "high Roman fashion."

This tragedy observes the classic unities of time and place. A hall in the Prefect's palace is made to cover its entire action, which occupies only one day. In its earnest pitch and lack of sprightly underplot, it also is Greek or Italian. Not long ago, listening to Salvini in "Samson" and other plays, I was struck by their likeness, in simplicity of action and costume, to the antique dramas. The actors were sufficient to themselves, and the audience was intent upon their lofty speech and passion; there was no lack of interest, but a refreshing spiritual elevation. The Gothic method better suits the English stage, nevertheless we need not refuse to profit by the experience of other lands. Our poetry, like the language, should draw its riches from all tongues and races, and well can endure a larger infusion of the ancient grandeur and simplicity. In the play before us Browning has but renewed the debt, long since incurred, of English literature to the Italian,—greater than that to all other sources combined. Not without reason, in "De Gustibus," he sang,—

> "Open my heart and you will see,
> Graved inside of it, 'Italy.'
> Such lovers old are I and she ;
> So it always was, so it still shall be !"

"King Victor," is one of those conventional plays in which he appears to ordinary advantage. His three dramatic masterpieces are "Pippa Passes," "A Blot in the 'Scutcheon." and "Colombe's Birthday."

The last-named play, inscribed to Barry Cornwall, really is a fresh and lovely little drama. The fair young heroine has possessed her duchy for a

2

single year, and now, upon her birthday, as she unsuspectingly awaits the greetings of her courtiers, is called upon to surrender her inheritance to Prince Berthold, decreed to be the lawful heir. At the same time Valence, a poor advocate of Cleves, seeks audience in behalf of his suffering townsmen, and ends by defending the Duchess's title to her rank. She loves him, and is so impressed by his nobility and courage as to decline the hand of the Prince, and surrender her duchy, to become the wife of Valence, with whom she joyfully retires to the ruined castle where her youth was spent. This play might be performed to the great interest of an audience composed exclusively of intellectual persons, who could follow the elaborate dialogue and would be charmed with its poetry and subtle thought. Once accept the manner of Browning, and you must be pleased with the delineation of the characters. "Colombe" herself is exquisite, and like one of Shakespeare's women. Valence seems too harsh and dry to win her, and her choice, despite his loyalty and intellect, is hardly defensible.

Still, "Colombe's Birthday" is the most natural and winsome of the author's stage-plays.

"A Blot in the 'Scutcheon" was brought out at Drury Lane, in 1843, and failed. This of course, for there is little in it to relieve the human spirit,— which cannot bear too much of earnestness and woe added•to the mystery and burden of our daily lives. Yet the piece has such tragic strength as to stamp the author as a great poet, though in a narrow range. One almost forgets the singular improbabilities of the story, the *blasé* talk of the child-lovers (an English Juliet of fourteen is against nature), the stiff language of the retainers, and various other blemishes. There is a serenade in which, unchecked by his fear of detection, Mertoun is made to sing under Mildred's window, —

" There's a woman like the dew drop, she's so purer than the purest !"

This song, composed seven years before the poet's meeting with Miss Barrett, is precisely in the style of "Lady Geraldine's Courtship," and other ballads of the gifted woman who became his wife.

The most simple and varied of his plays — that which shows every side of his genius, has most lightness and strength, and all in all may be termed a representative poem — is the beautiful drama with the quaint title of " Pippa Passes." It is a cluster of four scenes, with prologue, epilogue, and interludes ; half prose, half poetry, varying with the refinement of the dialogue. Pippa is a delicately pure, good, blithesome, peasant-maid. "'Tis but a little black-eyed, pretty, singing Felippa, gay silk-winding girl," — though with token, ere the end, that she is the child of a nobleman, put out of the way by a villain, Maffeo, at instigation of the next heir. Pippa knows nothing of this, but is piously content with her life of toil. It is New Year's Day at Asolo. She springs from bed, in her garret chamber, at sunrise, — resolved to enjoy to the full her sole holiday : she will not "squander a wavelet" of it, not a "mite of her twelve hours' treasure." Others can be happy throughout the year : haughty Ottima and Sebald, the lovers on the hill ; Jules and Phene, the artist and his bride ; Luigi and his mother ; Monsignor, the Bishop ; but Pippa has only this one day to enjoy. She envies these great ones a little, but reflects that God's love is best, after all. And yet, how little can she do ! How can she possibly affect the world ? Thus she muses, and goes out, singing, to her holiday and the sunshine. Now, it so happens that she passes, this day, each of the groups or persons we have named, at an important crisis in their lives, and they hear her various carols as she trills them forth in the innocent gladness of her heart. Sebald and Ottima have murdered the latter's aged husband, and are unremorseful in their guilty love. Jules is the victim of a fraud practised by his rival artists, who have put in his way a young girl, a paid model, whom he believes to be a pure and cultured maiden. He has married her, and just discovered the imposture. Luigi is hesitating whether to join a patriotic conspiracy. Monsignor is tempted by Maffeo to overlook his late brother's murder, for the sake of the estates, and to utterly ruin Pippa. The scene between Ottima and Sebald is the most intense and striking passage of all Browning's

poetry, and, possibly, of any dramatic verse composed during his lifetime up to the date of this play.
A passionate esoteric theme is treated with such
vigor and skill as to free it from any debasing taint,
in the dialogue from which I quote : —

> " *Ottima.* . . The past, would you give up the past
> Such as it is, pleasure and crime together ?
> Give up that noon I owned my love for you —
> The garden's silence — even the single bee,
> Persisting in his toil, suddenly stopt,
> And where he hid you only could surmise
> By some campanula's chalice set a-swing
> As he clung there — ' Yes, I love you ! '
>   *Sebald.*   And I drew
> Back ; put far back your face with both my hands
> Lest you should grow too full of me — your face
> So seemed athirst for my whole soul and body !
>
> .   .   .   .   .   .
>
> *Ottima.*   Then our crowning night —
> *Sebald.*   The July night ?
> *Ottima.*   The day of it too, Sebald !
> When the heaven's pillars seemed o'erbowed with heat,
> Its black blue canopy seemed let descend
> Close on us both, to weigh down each to each,
> And smother up all life except our life
> So lay we till the storm came.
>   *Sebald.*   How it came !

Ottima.   Buried in woods we lay, you recollect
Swift ran the searching tempest overhead ;
And ever and anon some bright white shaft
Burnt thro' the pine-tree roof,—here burnt and there,
As if God's messenger thro' the close wood screen
Plunged and replunged his weapon at a venture,
Feeling for guilty thee and me : then broke
The thunder like a whole sea overhead—
    Sebald.   Yes !

    .   .   .   .   .
                          How did we ever rise?
Was it that we slept? Why did it end?
    Ottima.   I felt you,
Fresh tapering to a point the ruffled ends
Of my loose locks 'twixt both your humid lips —
(My hair is fallen now — knot it again !)
    Sebald.   I kiss you now, dear Ottima, now, and now !
This way ? Will you forgive me — be once more
My great queen ?
    Ottima.   Bind it thrice about my brow ;
Crown me your queen, your spirit's arbitress,
Magnificent in sin.   Say that !
    Sebald.   I crown you
My great white queen, my spirit's arbitress,
Magnificent — "

But here Pippa passes, singing

        " God's in his heaven,—
          All's right with the world !"

Sebald is stricken with fear and remorse ; his para-
mour becomes hideous in his eyes ; he bids her
dress her shoulders, wipe off that paint, and leave
him, for he hates her ! She, the woman, is at least
true to her lover, and prays God to be merciful, not
to her, but to him.

The scene changes to the post-nuptial meeting of
Jules and Phene, and then in succession to the
other passages and characters we have mentioned.
All these persons are vitally affected,— have their
lives changed, merely by Pippa's weird and
suggestive songs, coming, as if by accident, upon
their hearing at that critical moment. With certain
reservations this is a strong and delicate conception,
admirably worked out.   The usual fault is present :
the characters, whether students, peasants, or
soldiers, all talk like sages ; Pippa reasons like a
Paracelsus in pantalets,— her intellectual songs are
strangely put in the mouth of an ignorant silk-
winding girl ; Phene is more natural, though mature,
even for Italy, at fourteen. Browning's children are
old as himself ; — he rarely sees them objectively.

Even in the songs he is awkward, void of lyric grace ; if they have the wilding flavor, they have more than need be of specks and gnarledness. In the epilogue Pippa seeks her garret, and, as she disrobes, after artlessly running over the events of her holiday, soliloquizes thus : —

> " Now, one thing I should like really to know:
> How near I ever might approach all these
> I only fancied being, this long day —
> — Approach, I mean, so as to touch them — so
> As to .. in some way .. move them — if you please,
> Do good or evil to them some slight way. "

Finally, she sleeps,— unconscious of her day's mission,— and of the fact that her own life is to be something more than it has been,— but not until she has murmured these words of a hymn : —

> "All service is the same with God,—
> With God, whose puppets, best and worst,
> Are we : there is no last nor first."

"Pippa Passes" is a work of pure art, and has a wealth of original fancy and romance, apart from

its wisdom, to which every poet will do justice. Its
faults are those of style and undue intellectuality.
To quote the author's words, in another drama,

" Ah? well ! he o'er-refines,— the scholar's fault ! '

As it is, we accept his work, looking upon it as upon some treasured yet *bizarre* painting of the mixed
school, whose beauties are the more striking for its
defects. The former are inherent, the latter exter-
nal and subordinate.

Everything from this poet is, or used to be, of
value and interest, and "A Soul's Tragedy"
is of both : first, for a masterly distinction
between the action of sentiment and that founded
on principle, and, secondly, for wit, satire, and
knowledge of affairs. Ogniben, the Legate, is the
most thorough man of the world Browning has
drawn. That is a matchless stroke, at the close,
where he says: " I have seen four-and-twenty leaders
of revolts." It is a consolation to recall this when
a pretender arises ; his race is measured,— his fall
shall surely come.

With "Luria," thirty years ago, Browning, whose stage-plays had been failures, and whose closet-dramas had found too small a reading, made his "last attempt, for the present, at dramatic poetry." It remains to examine his miscellaneous after-work, including the long poems which have appeared within the last five years,— the most prolific, if not the most creative, period of his untiring life.

V.

Something of a dramatic character pertains to nearly all of Browning's lyrics. Like his wife, he has preferred to study human hearts rather than the forms of nature. A note to the first collection of his briefer poems places them under the head of Dramatic Pieces. This was at a time when English poets were enslaved to the idyllic method, and forgot that their readers had passions most suggestive to art when exalted above the tranquillity of picturesque repose. Herein Browning justly may claim originality. Even the Laureate combined the art of Keats with the contemplative habit of Words-

worth, and adapted them to his own times ; while
Browning was the prophet of that reaction which
holds that the proper study of mankind is man.
His effort, weak or able, was at figure-painting, in
distinction from that of landscape or still life. It
has not flourished during the recent period, but we
are indebted to him for what we have of it. In an
adverse time it was natural for it to assume peculiar,
almost morbid phases ; but of this struggling, turbid
figure-school,— variously represented by the younger Lytton, Rossetti, Swinburne, and others, he was
the long-neglected progenitor. His genius may
have been unequal to his aims. It is not easy for
him to combine a score of figures upon the ample
canvas : his work is at its best in separated ideals,
or, rather, in portraits,— his dramatic talent being
more realistic than imaginative. Still, portraiture,
in a certain sense, is the highest form of painting,
and Browning's personal studies must not be under-
valued. As usual, even here he is unequal, and,
while some of them are matchless, in others, like all
men of genius who aim at the highest, he conspicu-

ously fails. A man of talent may never fail, yet never rise above a fixed height. Yet if Browning were a man of great genius his failures would not so outnumber his successes that half his lyrics could be missed without injury to his reputation.

The shorter pieces, "Dramatic Romances and Lyrics," in the first general collection of his works, are of a better average grade than those in his latest book of miscellanies. One of the best is "My Last Duchess," a masterly sketch, comprising within sixty lines enough matter to furnish Browning, nowadays, with an excuse for a quarto. Nothing can be subtler than the art whereby the Duke is made to reveal a cruel tragedy of which he was the relentless villain, to betray the blackness of his heart, and to suggest a companion-tragedy in his betrothal close at hand. Thus was introduced a new method, applied with such coolness as to suggest the idea of vivisection or morbid anatomy.

But let us group other lyrics in this collection with the matter of two later volumes, *Men and Women*, and *Dramatis Personæ*. These books, made

up of isolated poems, contain the bulk of his work
during the eighteen years which followed his marriage in 1846. While their contents include no long
poem or drama, they seem, upon the whole, to be
the fullest expression of his genius, and that for which
he is likeliest to be remembered. Every poet has
limitations, and in such briefer studies Browning
keeps within the narrowest bounds allotted to him.
Very few of his best pieces are in " Dramatis Personæ," the greater part of which book is made up
of his most ragged, uncouth, and even puerile verse ;
and it is curious that it appeared at a time when his
wife was scribbling the rhetorical verse of those
years which I have designated as her period of
decline. But observe the general excellence of the
fifty poems in " Men and Women,"— collected nine
years earlier, when the author was forty years old,
and at his prime. In the chapter upon Tennyson
it was stated that almost every poet has a representative book, showing him at full height and variety.
"Men and Women," like the Laureate's volume of
1842, is the most finished and comprehensive of the

author's works, and the one his readers least could spare. Here we find numbers of those thrilling, skilfully dramatic studies, which so many have imitated without catching the secret of their power.

The general effect of Browning's miscellaneous poems is like that of a picture-gallery, where cabinet paintings, by old and modern masters, are placed at random upon the walls. Some are rich in color; others, strong in light and shade. A few are elaborately finished,—more are careless drawings, fresh, but hurriedly sketched in. Often the subjects are repulsive, but occasionally we have the solitary, impressive figure of a lover or a saint.

The poet is as familiar with mediæval thought and story as most authors with their own time, and adapts them to his lyrical uses. "Andrea del Sarto" belongs to the same group with " My Last Duchess." It is the language of " the faultless painter," addressed to his beautiful and thoughtless wife, for whom he has lowered his ideal — and from whose chains he cannot break, though he knows she is unworthy, and even false to him. He moans before one of

Raphael's drawings, excusing the faults, in envy of
the genius : —

> "Still, what an arm ! and I could alter it.
>   But all the play, the insight and the stretch —
>   Out of me ! out of me !   And wherefore out ?
>   Had you enjoined them on me, given me soul,
>   We might have risen to Raphael, I and you.
>
> .   .   .   .   .   .
>
>   But had you — O, with the same perfect brow,
>   And perfect eyes, and more than perfect mouth,
>   And the low voice my soul hears, as a bird
>   The fowler's pipe, and follows to the snare,—
>   Had you, with these the same, but brought a mind !
>   Some women do so.   Had the mouth there urged
>   'God and the glory ! never care for gain ! '
>
> .   .   .   .   .   .
>
>   I might have done it for you."

Were it indeed "all for love," then were the
"world well lost"; but even while he dallies with
his wife she listens for her gallant's signal.   This
poem is one of Browning's finest studies : of late he
has given us nothing equal to it.   The picture of
the rollicking " Fra Lippo Lippi " is broad, free-
handed, yet scarcely so well done.   " Pictor Igno-
tus " is upon another art-theme, and in quiet beauty

differs from the poet's usual manner. Other old-time studies, good and poor, which served to set the fashion for a number of minor poets, are such pieces as "Count Gismond," "Cristina," "The Laboratory," and "The Confessional."

How perilous an easy rhymed-metre is to this author was discernible in "Sordello." After the same manner he is tempted to garrulity in the semi-religious poems, "Christmas Eve" and "Easter Day." It is difficult otherwise to account for their dreary flow, since they are no more original in theology than poetical in language and design.

It would be strange if Browning were not indebted, for some of his most powerful themes, to the superstition from which mediæval art, politics, and daily life took their prevailing tone. In his analysis of its quality he seems to me extremely profound. Monasticism in Spain even now is not so different from that of the fifteenth century, and the repulsive imagery of a piece like the "Soliloquy of the Spanish Cloister," written in the harshest verse, well consorts with a period when the orders,

4

that took their origin in exalted purity, had become degraded through lust, gluttony, jealousy, and every cardinal sin. Browning draws his monks, as Doré in the illustrations to "Les Contes Drôlatiques," with porcine or wolfish faces, monstrous, seamed with vice, defiled in body and soul. "The Bishop orders his Tomb" has been criticised as not being a faithful study of the Romish ecclesiastic, A. D. 15— ; but, unless I misapprehend the spirit of that period, this is one of the poet's strongest portraitures. Religion then was often a compound of fear, bigotry, and greed ; its officers, trained in the Church, seemed to themselves invested with something greater than themselves ; their ideas of good and evil, after years of ritualistic service,— made gross with pelf, jealousy, sensualism, and even blood-guiltiness,— became strangely intermixed. The poet overlays this groundwork with that love of art and luxury — of jasper, peach-blossom marble, and lazuli — inbred in every Italian,— and even with the scholar's desire to have his epitaph carved aright : —

" Choice Latin, picked phrase, Tully's every word,
  No gaudy ware like Gandolf's second line,—
  Tully, my masters?   Ulpian serves his need !
  And then how I shall lie through centuries,
  And hear the blessed mutter of the mass,
  And see God made and eaten all day long,
  And feel the steady candle-flame, and taste
  Good, strong, thick, stupefying incense-smoke ! "

All this commanded to his bastards !   And for the rest, were ever suspicion, hatred, delight at outwitting a rival in love and preferment, and every other loathsome passion strong in death, more ruthlessly and truthfully depicted ?

Of strictly mediæval church studies, "The Heretic's Tragedy" and "Holy-Cross Day," with their grotesque diction, annotations, and prefixes, are the most skilful reproductions essayed in our time. Browning alone could have conceived or written them.   In "A Grammarian's Funeral," "Abt Vogler," and "Master Hugues," early scholarship and music are commemorated.   The language of the simplest of these is so intricate that we have to be educated in a new tongue to comprehend them.

Their value lies in the human nature revealed under such fantastic, and, to us, unnatural aspects developed in other times.

"Artemis Prologuizes," the poet's antique sketch, is as unclassical as one might expect from its affected title. "Saul," a finer poem, may have furnished hints to Swinburne with respect to anapestic verse and the Hebraic feeling. Three poems, which strive to reproduce the early likeness and spirit of Christianity, merit close attention. One describes the raising of Lazarus, narrated in an "Epistle of Karshish, the Arab Physician." The pious, learned mage sees in the miracle

> "But a case of mania — subinduced
> By epilepsy, at the turning-point
> Of trance prolonged unduly some three days."

"Cleon" is an exposition of the highest ground reached by the Pagan philosophy, set forth in a letter written, by a wise poet, to Protos, the King. At the end he makes light of the preachings of Paul, who is welcome to the few proselytes he can make among the ignorant slaves : —

" And (as I gathered from a bystander)
Their doctrines could be held by no sane man."

The reader is forced to stop and consider what despised doctrines even now may be afloat, which in time may constitute the whole world's creed. The most elaborate of these pieces is " A Death in the Desert," the last words of St. John, the Evangelist, recorded by Pamphylax, an Antiochene martyr. The prologue and epilogue are sufficiently pedantic, but, like the long-drawn narrative, so characteristic, that this curious production may be taken as a representative poem. A similar bit of realism is the sketch of a great poet, seen in every-day life by a fellow-townsman, entitled, " How it Strikes a Contemporary." And now, having selected a few of these miscellaneous pieces to represent the mass, how shall we define their true value, and their influence upon recent art ?

Browning is justified in offering such works as a substitute for poetic treatment of English themes, since he is upon ground naturally his own. Yet as poems they fail to move us, and to gloriously elevate the soul, but are the outgrowth of minute realism and speculation. To quote from one who is reviewing a kindred sort of literature, they sin, "against the spirit of antiquity, in carrying back the modern analytic feeling to a scene where it does not belong." It is owing precisely to this sin that several of Browning's longer works are literary and rhythmical prodigies, monuments of learning and labor rather than ennobling efforts of the imagination. His hand is burdened by too great accumulation of details,— and then there is the ever-present spirit of Robert Browning peering from the eyes of each likeness, however faithful, that he portrays.

He is the most intellectual of poets, Tennyson not excepted. Take, for example, "Caliban," with its text, "Thou thoughtest I was altogether such an one as thyself." The motive is a study of anthropomorphism, by reflection of its counterpart in a lower animal, half man, half beast, possessed of the faculty of speech. The "natural theology" is food for thought ; the poetry, descriptive and otherwise,

realism carried to such perfection as to seem imagination. Here we have Browning's curious reasoning
at its best. But what can be more vulgar and
strictly unpoetical than " Mr. Sludge, the Medium,"
a composition of the same period ? Our familiarity
with such types as those to which the author's
method is here applied enables us to test it with anything but satisfaction. Applied to a finer subject,
in " Bishop Blougram's Apology," we heartily
admire its virile analysis of the motives actuating
the great prelate, who after due reflection has
rejected

> " A life of doubt diversified by faith
> For one of faith diversified by doubt."

Cardinal Wiseman is worldly and insincere ; the
poet, Gigadibs, is earnest and on the right side ; yet,
somehow, we do not quite despise the churchman
nor admire the poet. This piece is at once the
foremost defence and arraignment of Philistinism,
drawn up by a thinker broad enough to comprehend
both sides. As an intellectual work, it is meat and

wine ; as a poem, as a thing of beauty,—but that is quite another point in issue.

Browning's offhand, occasional lyrics, such as "Waring," "Time's Revenges," "Up in a Villa," "The Italian in England," "By the Fireside," "The Worst of It," etc., are suggestive, and some of them widely familiar. His style has been caught by others. The picturesqueness and easy rhythm of "The Flight of the Duchess," and the touches in briefer lyrics, are repeated by minnesingers like Owen Meredith and Dobell. There is a grace and turn that still evades them, for sometimes their master can be as sweet and tuneful as Lodge, or any other of the skylarks. Witness "In a Gondola," that delicious Venetian cantata, full of music and sweet sorrow, or "One Way of Love," for example, —but such melodies are none too frequent. When he paints nature, as in "Home Thoughts, from Abroad," how fresh and fine the landscape !

> "And after April, when May follows,
> And the white-throat builds, and all the swallows,—
> Hark ! where my blossomed pear-tree in the hedge

Leans to the field and scatters on the clover
Blossoms, and dew-drops — at the bent spray's edge —
That's the wise thrush ; he sings each song twice over
Lest you should think he never could recapture
The first fine careless rapture !"

Having in mind Shakespeare and Shelley, I nevertheless think the last three lines the finest ever written touching the song of a bird.   Contrast therewith the poet's later method,— the prose-run-mad
of stanzas such as this : —

"Hobbs hints blue,— straight he turtle eats.
Nobbs prints blue,— claret crowns his cup.
Nokes outdares Stokes in azure feats,—
Both gorge.   Who fished the murex up?
What porridge had John Keats ?"

And this by no means the most impertinent of
kindred verses in his books,— poetry that neither
gods nor men can endure or understand, and yet
interstrewn with delicate trifles, such as "Mem-
orabilia," which for *suggestiveness* long will be
preserved.   Who so deft to catch the one immortal
moment, the fleeting exquisite word ?   Who so wont
to reach for it, and wholly fail ?

VI.

We come, at last, to a class of Browning's poems
that I have grouped for their expression of that
dominating sentiment, to which reference was made
at the beginning of this review. Their moral is
that of the apothegm that " Attractions are propor-
tional to destinies " ; of rationalistic freedom, as
opposed to Calvinism ; of a belief that the greatest
sin does not consist in giving rein to our desires,
but in stinting or too prudently repressing them.
Life must have its full and free development.   And,
as love is the master-passion, he is most earnest in
illustrating this belief from its good or evil progress,
and to this end has composed his most impressive
verse.

A main lesson of Browning's emotional poetry is
that the unpardonable sin is "to dare something
against nature."   To set bounds to love is to com-
mit that sin.   Through his instinct for conditions
which engender the most dramatic forms of speech
and action, he is, at least, as an artist, tolerant of

what is called an intrigue ; and that many com-
placent English and American readers do not recognize this, speaks volumes either for their stupidity,
or for their hypocrisy and inward sympathy in a
creed which they profess to abhor. Affecting to
comprehend and admire Browning, they still refuse
to forgive Swinburne,— whose crude earlier poems
brought the lust of the flesh to the edge of a gross-
ness too palpable to be seductive, and from which
his riper manhood has departed altogether. The
elder poet, from first to last, has appeared to defend
the elective affinities against impediments of law
theology, or social rank. It is not my province to
discuss the ethics of this matter, but simply to speak
of it as a fact.

It will not do to fall back upon Browning's pro-
test, in the note to his " Dramatic Lyrics," that
these are " so many utterances of so many imaginary
persons," and not his own. For when he returns
persistently to a certain theme, illustrates it in
divers ways, and heaps the coals of genius upon it
till it breaks out into flame, he ceases to be objective

and reveals his secret thought. No matter how
conservative his habit, he is to be judged, like any
artist, by his work ; and in all his poems we see a
taste for the joys and sorrows of a free, irresponsible
life,— like that of the Italian lovers, of students in
their vagrant youth, or of Consuelo and her husband upon the windy heath. Above all, he tells
us : —

> "Thou shalt know, those arms once curled
>   About thee, what we knew before,
>   How love is the only good in the world."

"In a Balcony" is the longest and finest of his
emotional poems : a dramatic episode, in three dia-
logues, the personages of which talk at too great
length,— although, no doubt, many and varied
thoughts flash through the mind at supreme
moments, and it is Browning's custom to put them
all upon the record. How clearly the story is
wrought ! What exquisite language, and passion
triumphant over life and death ! Mark the transformation of the lonely queen, in the one radiant
hour of her life that tells her she is beloved, and

makes her an angel of goodness and light. She barters power and pride for love, clutching at this one thing as at Heaven, and feels

" How soon a smile of God can change the world."

Then comes the transformation, upon discovery of the cruel deceit,— her vengeance and despair. The love of Constance, who for it will surrender life, and even Norbert's hand, is more unselfish ; never more subtly, perhaps, than in this poem, has been illustrated Byron's epigram : —

"In her first passion, woman loves her lover
In all the others, all she loves is love."

Here, too, is the profound lesson of the whole, that a word of the man Norbert's simple, blundering truth would have prevented all this coil. But the poet is at his height in treating of the master passion : —

" Remember, I (and what am I to you ?)
Would give up all for one, leave throne, lose life,
Do all but just unlove him ! he loves me."

With fine abandonment he makes the real worth
so much more than the ideal : —

> " We live, and they experiment on life,
>   These poets, painters, all who stand aloof
>   To overlook the farther. Let us be
>   The thing they look at ! "

But in a large variety of minor lyrics it is hinted
that our instincts have something divine about
them ; that, regardless of other obligations, we may
not disobey the inward monition. A man not only
may forsake father and mother and cleave to his
wife ; but forsake his wife and cleave to the pre-
destined one. No sin like repression ; no sting like
regret ; no requital for the opportunity slighted and
gone by. In "The Statue and the Bust,"—a typi-
cal piece,— had the man and woman seen clearly
"the end " of life, though "a crime," they had not
so failed of it : —

> " If you choose to play — is my principle !
>   Let a man contend to the uttermost
>   For his life's set prize, be it what it will !

" The counter our lovers staked was lost
  As surely as if it were lawful coin :
  And the sin I impute to each frustrate ghost

" Was, the unlit lamp and the ungirt loin.
  Though the end in sight was a crime, I say."

"A Light Woman" turns upon the right of every soul, however despicable, to its own happiness, and to freedom from the meddling of others. The words of many lyrics, attesting the boundless liberty and sovereignty of love, are plainly written, and to say the lesson is not there is to ape those commentators who discover an allegorical meaning in each Scriptural text that interferes with their special creeds.

Both Browning and his wife possessed by nature a radical gift for sifting things to the core, an heroic disregard of every conventional gloss or institution. They were thoroughly mated in this respect, though one may have outstripped the other in exercise of the faculty. Their union, apparently, was so absolute that neither felt any need of fuller emotional life. The sentiment of Browning's pas-

sional verse, therefore, is not the outgrowth of perceptions sharpened by restraint. The poetry
addressed to his wife is, if anything, of a still higher order.   He watches her

> " Reading by firelight, that great brow
>   And the spirit-small hand propping it
>   Mutely—my heart knows how—
>
> " When, if I think but deep enough,
>   You are wont to answer, prompt as rhyme";

and again and again addresses her in such lines as
these : —

> " God be thanked, the meanest of his creatures
>   Boasts two soul-sides, one to face the world with,
>   One to show a woman when he loves her.
>
> This to you — yourself my moon of poets !
> Ah, but that's the world's side — there's the wonder —
> Thus they see you, praise you, think they know you."

In fine, not only his passional lyrics, but all the
poems relating to the wedded love in which his own
deepest instincts were thoroughly gratified, are the
most strong and simple portion of his verse,— show-

ing that luminous expression is still the product of high emotion, as some conceive the diamond to have been crystallized by the electric shock.

VII.

Many of the lyrics in the volume of 1864* are so thin and faulty, and so fail to carry out the author's intent,— the one great failure in art,— as sadly to illustrate the progressive ills which attend upon a wrong method.

The gift still remained, however, for no work displays more of ill-diffused power and swift application than Browning's longest poem, *The Ring and the Book.* It has been succeeded rapidly, within five years, by other works,— the whole almost equalling, in bulk, the entire volume of his former writings. Their special quality is affluence : limitless wealth of language and illustration. They abound in the material of poetry. A poet should condense from such star-dust the orbs which give light and outlast time. As in "Sordello," Browning

---

* *" Dramatis Personæ."*

again fails to do this ; he gives us his first draught, — the huge, outlined block, yet to be reduced to fit proportions,— the painter's sketch, blotchy and too obscure, and of late without the early freshness.

Nevertheless, " The Ring and the Book " is a wonderful production, the extreme of realistic art, and considered, not without reason, by the poet's admirers, to be his greatest work. To review it would require a special chapter, and I have said enough with respect to the author's style in my citation of his less extended poems ; but as the product of sheer intellect this surpasses them all. It is the story of a tragedy which took place at Rome one hundred and seventy years ago. The poet seems to have found his thesis in an old book,— part print, part manuscript,— bought for eight pence at a Florence stall : —

> " A book in shape, but, really, pure crude fact
> Secreted from man's life when hearts beat hard,
> And brains, high-blooded, ticked two centuries since."

The versified narrative of the child Pampilia's sale to Count Guido, of his cruelty and violence, of her rescue by a young priest,— the pursuit, the lawful separation, the murder by Guido of the girl and her putative parents, the trial and condemnation of the murderer, and the affirmation of his sentence by the Pope,— all this is made to fill out a poem of twenty-one thousand lines ; but these include ten different versions of the same tale, besides the poet's prelude, — in which latter he gives a general outline of it, so that the reader plainly may understand it, and the historian then be privileged to wander as he choose.

The chapters which contain the statements of the priest-lover and Pampilia are full of tragic beauty and emotion ; the Pope's soliloquy, though too pro-longed, is a wonderful piece of literary metempsy-chosis ; but the speeches of the opposing lawyers carry realism to an intolerable, prosaic extreme. Each of these books, possibly, should be read by itself, and not too steadily nor too often. Observe that the author, in elevated passages, sometimes for-gets his usual manner and breaks into the cadences of Tennyson's style ; for instance, the apostrophe to his dead wife, beginning

" O lyric Love, half angel and half bird,
    And all a wonder and a wild desire ! "

But elsewhere he leads the reaction from the art-
school. His presentations are endless : in his
architecture the tracery, scroll-work, and multifoil
bewilder us and divert attention from the main
design. Yet in presence of the changeful flow of
his verse, and the facility wherewith he records the
speculations of his various characters, we are struck
with wonder. "The Ring and the Book" is thus
far imaginative, and a rhythmical marvel, but is it a
stronghold of poetic art? As a whole, we cannot
admit that it is ; and yet the thought, the vocab-
ulary, imagery, the wisdom, lavished upon this story,
would equip a score of ordinary writers, and place
them beyond danger of neglect.

Balaustion's Adventure, the poet's next volume,
displays a tranquil beauty uncommon in his verse,
and it seems as if he sought, after his most prolonged
effort, to refresh his mind with the sweetness and
repose of Greek art. He treads decently and rever-
ently in the buskins of Euripides, and forgets to be

garrulous in his chaste semi-translation of the Alcestis. The girl Balaustion's prelude and conclusion are very neatly turned, reminding us of Landor ; nor does the book, as a whole, lack the antique flavor and the blue, laughing freshness of the Trinacrian sea.

What shall be said of *Fifine at the Fair*, or of that volume, the last but one of Browning's essays, which not long ago succeeded it ? Certainly, that they exhibit his steadfast tendency to produce work that is less and less poetical. There is no harder reading than the first of these poems ; no more badly chosen, rudely handled measure than the verse selected for it ; no pretentious work, from so great a pen, has less of the spirit of grace and comeliness. It is a pity that the author has not somewhat accustomed himself to write in prose, for he insists upon recording all of his thoughts, and many of them are essentially prosaic. Strength and subtilty are not enough in art : beauty, either of the fair, the terrible, or the grotesque, is its justification, and a poem that repels at the outset has small excuse for being. "Prince Hohenstiel-Schwan-gau, Savior of Society," is another of Browning's experiments in vivisection, the subject readily made out to be the late Emperor of the French. It is longer than "Bishop Blougram's Apology," but compare it therewith, and we are forced to perceive a decline in terseness, virility, and true imaginative power.

Red Cotton Night-Cap Country; or, Turf and Towers,—what exasperating titles Browning puts forth ! this time under the protection of Miss Thack-eray. That the habit is inbred, however, is proved by some absurd invention whenever it becomes necessary to coin a proper name. After "Blup-hocks" and "Gigadibs," we have no right to com-plain of the title of his Breton romance. The poem itself contains a melo-dramatic story, and hence is less uninteresting than "Fifine." But to have such a volume, after Browning's finer works, come out with each revolving year, is enough to ex-tort from his warmest admirers the cry of "Words ! Words ! Words !" Much of the detail is paltry,

and altogether local or temporal, so that it will become inexplicable fifty years hence. There is a
constant "dropping into" prose ; moreover, whole
pages of wandering nonsense are called forth by
some word, like "night-cap" or "fiddle," taken for
a text, as if to show the poet's mastery of verse-
building and how contemptible he can make it. Once
he would have put the narrative of this poem into a
brief dramatic sketch that would have had beauty
and interest. "My Last Duchess" is a more
genuine addition to literature than the two hundred
pages of this tedious and affected romance. A prolonged career has not been of advantage to the
reputation of Browning : his tree was well-rooted
and reached a sturdy growth, but the yield is too
profuse, of a fruit that still grows sourer from year
to year.

Nevertheless, this poet, like all men of genius, has
happy seasons in which, by some remarkable per-
formance, he seems to renew his prime. *Aristopha-
nes' Apology* continues the charm of "Balaustion's
Adventure," to which poem it is a sequel. What I

have said of the classical purity and sweetness of the earlier production will apply to portions of " the last adventure of Balaustion,"— which also includes " a transcript from Euripides." Besides, it displays the richness of scholarship, command of learned details, skill in sophistry and analysis, power to re-call, awaken, and dramatically inform the historic past, in all which qualifications this master still remains unequalled by any modern writer, even by the most gifted and affluent pupil of his own impres-sive school.

VIII.

A fair estimate of Browning may, I think, be de-duced from the foregoing review of his career. It is hard to speak of one whose verse is a metrical paradox. I have called him the most original and the most unequal of living poets ; he continually descends to a prosaic level, but at times is elevated to the Laureate's highest flights. Without realizing the proper function of art, he nevertheless sympa-thizes with the joyous liberty of its devotees ; his

life may be conventional, but he never forgets the
Latin Quarter, and often celebrates that freedom in
love and song which is the soul of Béranger's

> " Dans un grenier qu'on est bien a vingt ans."

then, too, what working man of letters does not
thank him when he says,—

> "But you are of the trade, my Puccio !
> You have the fellow-craftsman's sympathy.
> There's none knows like a fellow of the craft
> The all unestimated sum of pains
> That go to a success the world can see."

He is an eclectic, and will not be restricted in his
themes ; on the other hand, he gives us too gross a
mixture of poetry, fact, and metaphysics, appearing
to have no sense of composite harmony, but to revel
in arabesque strangeness and confusion.   He has a
barbaric sense of color and lack of form.   Striving
against the trammels of verse, he really is far less a
master of expression than others who make less
resistance.   We read in " Pippa Passes ": " If there
should arise a new painter, will it not be in some

such way by a poet, now, or a musician (spirits who have conceived and perfected an Ideal through some other channel), transferring it to this, and escaping our conventional roads by pure ignorance of them?" This is the Pre-Raphaelite idea, and, so far, good ; but Browning's fault is that, if he has "conceived," he certainly has made no effort to "perfect" an Ideal.

And here I wish to say,— and this is something which, soon or late, every thoughtful poet must discover,— that the structural exigencies of art, if one adapts his genius to them, have a beneficent reaction upon the artist's original design. By some friendly law they help the work to higher excellence, suggesting unthought-of touches, and refracting, so to speak, the single beam of light in rays of varied and delightful beauty.

The brakes which art applies to the poet's movement not only regulate, but strengthen its progress. Their absence is painfully evinced by the mass of Browning's unread verse. Works like "Sordello" and "Fifine," however intellectual, seem, like the

removal of the Malvern Hills, a melancholy waste
of human power. When some romance like the
last-named comes from his pen, — an addition in
volume, not in quality, to what he has done before,
— I feel a sadness like that engendered among hun-
dreds of gloomy folios in some black-letter alcove :
books, forever closed, over which the mighty monks
of old wore out their lives, debating minute points
of casuistic theology, though now the very memory
of their discussions has passed away. Would that
Browning might take to heart his own words,
addressed, in "Transcendentalism," to a brother-
poet : —

> "Song's our art :
> Whereas you please to speak these naked thoughts
> Instead of draping them in sights and sounds.
> — True thoughts, good thoughts, thoughts fit to treasure up !
> But why such long prolusion and display,
> Such turning and adjustment of the harp ?
>
> .   .   .   .
>
> But here's your fault; grown men want thought, you think ;
> Thought's what they mean by verse, and seek in verse :
> Boys seek for images and melody,
> Men must have reason,— so you aim at men.
> Quite otherwise !"

Incidentally we have noted the distinction between the drama of Browning and that of the absolute kind, observing that his characters reflect his
own mental traits, and that their action and emotion
are of small moment compared with the speculations
to which he makes them all give voice. Still, he
has dramatic insight, and a minute power of reading
other men's hearts. His moral sentiment has a
potent and subtile quality :—through his early poems
he really founded a school, and had imitators, and
although of his later method there are none, the
younger poets whom he has most affected very
naturally began work by carrying his philosophy to
a startling yet perfectly logical extreme.

Much of his poetry is either very great or very
poor. It has been compared to Wagner's music,
and entitled the "poetry of the future ;" but if this
be just, then we must revise our conception of what
poetry really is. The doubter incurs the contempt-
uous enmity of two classes of the dramatist's
admirers : first, of the metaphysical, who disregard
considerations of passion, melody, and form ;

secondly, of those who are sensitive to their master's failings, but, in view of his greatness, make it a point of honor to defend them. That greatness lies in his originality ; his error, arising from perverseness or congenital defect, is the violation of natural and beautiful laws. This renders his longer poems of less worth than his lyrical studies, while, through avoidance of it, productions, differing as widely as " The Eve of St. Agnes," and " In Memoriam," will outlive " The Ring and the Book." In writing of Arnold I cited his own quotation of Goethe's distinction between the dilettanti, who affect genius and despise art, and those who respect their calling though not gifted with high creative power. Browning escapes the limitations of the latter class, but incurs the reproach visited upon the former ; and by his contempt of beauty, or inability to surely express it, fails of that union of art and spiritual power which always characterizes a poet entirely great.

CAVALIER TUNES.

I.—MARCHING ALONG.

I.

Kentish Sir Byng stood for his King,
Bidding the crop-headed Parliament swing:
And, pressing a troop unable to stoop
And see the rogues flourish and honest folk droop,
Marched them along, fifty-score strong,
Great-hearted gentlemen, singing this song.

II.

God for King Charles ! Pym and such carles
To the Devil that prompts 'em their treasonous
    parles !
Cavaliers, up ! Lips from the cup,
Hands from the pasty, nor bite take nor sup
Till you're (*Chorus*) *marching along, fifty-score strong,*
Great-hearted gentlemen, singing this song.

78

III.

Hampden to Hell, and his obsequies' knell
Serve Hazelrig, Fiennes, and young Harry as well !
England, good cheer !   Rupert is near !
Kentish and loyalists, keep we not here

> (*Cho.*) *Marching along, fifty-score strong,*
> *Great-hearted gentlemen, singing this song ?*

IV.

Then, God for King Charles !   Pym and his snarls
To the Devil that pricks on such pestilent carles !
Hold by the right, you double your might ;
So, onward to Nottingham, fresh for the fight,

> (*Cho.*) *March we along, fifty-score strong,*
> *Great-hearted gentlemen, singing this song !*

II.— GIVE A ROUSE.

I.

King Charles, and who'll do him right now ?
King Charles, and who's ripe for fight now ?
Give a rouse : here's, in Hell's despite now,
King Charles !

II.

Who gave me the goods that went since?
Who raised me the house that sank once?
Who helped me to gold I spent since?
Who found me in wine you drank once?

> (*Cho.*) *King Charles, and who'll do him right now?*
> *King Charles, and who's ripe for fight now?*
> *Give a rouse : here's in Hell's despite now.*
> *King Charles !*

III.

To whom used my boy George quaff else,
By the old fool's side that begot him?
For whom did he cheer and laugh else,
While Noll's damned troopers shot him?

> (*Cho.*) *King Charles, and who'll do him right now?*
> *King Charles, and who's ripe for fight now?*
> *Give a rouse : here's in Hell's despite now,*
> *King Charles !*

III.— BOOT AND SADDLE.

I.

Boot, saddle, to horse, and away !
Rescue my Castle, before the hot day
Brightens to blue from its silvery gray,

        (Cho.) Boot, saddle, to horse, and away!

II.

Ride past the suburbs, asleep as you'd say ;
Many's the friend there will listen and pray
God's luck to gallants that strike up the lay,

        (Cho.) Boot, saddle, to horse, and away!

III.

Forty miles off, like a roebuck at bay,
Flouts Castle Brancepeth the Roundhead's array :
Who laughs, " Good fellows are these by my fay,

        (Cho.) Boot, saddle, to horse, and away?

6

IV.

Who? My wife Gertrude; that honest and gay,
Laughs when you talk of surrendering, " Nay !
I've better counsellors ; what counsel they ?

 (*Cho.*) " *Boot, saddle, to horse, and away !* "

"HOW THEY BROUGHT THE GOOD NEWS FROM GHENT TO AIX."

[16—.]

I.

I sprang to the stirrup, and Joris, and he ;
I galloped, Dirck galloped, we galloped all three ;
"Good speed !" cried the watch, as the gate-bolts
    undrew ;
"Speed !" echoed the wall to us galloping through ;
Behind shut the postern, the lights sank to rest,
And into the midnight we galloped abreast.

II.

Not a word to each other ; we kept the great pace
Neck by neck, stride by stride, never changing our
    place ;

83

I turned in my saddle and made its girths tight,
Then shortened each stirrup, and set the pique
　　right,
Rebuckled the cheek-strap, chained slacker the bit,
Nor galloped less steadily Roland a whit.

III.

'Twas moonset at starting ; but while we drew near
Lokeren, the cocks crew and twilight dawned clear ;
At Boom, a great yellow star came out to see ;
At Düffeld, 'twas morning as plain as could be ;
And from Mecheln church-steeple we heard the
　　half-chime,
So Joris broke silence with, " Yet there is time ! "

IV.

At Aerschot, up leaped of a sudden the sun,
And against him the cattle stood black every one,
To stare thro' the mist at us galloping past,
And I saw my stout galloper Roland at last,
With resolute shoulders, each butting away
The haze, as some bluff river headland its spray.

V.

And his low head and crest, just one sharp ear bent
  back
For my voice, and the other pricked out on his
  track ;
And one eye's black intelligence,— ever that glance
O'er its white edge at me, his own master, askance !
And the thick heavy spume-flakes which aye and
  anon
His fierce lips shook upwards in galloping on.

VI.

By Hasselt, Dirck groaned ; and cried Joris, "Stay
  spur !
" Your Roos galloped bravely, the fault's not in her,
" We'll remember at Aix "— for one heard the quick
  wheeze
Of her chest, saw the stretched neck and staggering
  knees,
And sunk tail, and horrible heave of the flank,
As down on her haunches she shuddered and sank.

VII.

So we were left galloping, Joris and I,
Past Looz and past Tongres, no cloud in the sky ;
The broad sun above laughed a pitiless laugh,
'Neath our feet broke the brittle bright stubble like
　　chaff ;
Till over by Dalhem a dome-spire sprang white,
And " Gallop," gasped Joris, " for Aix is in sight ! "

VIII.

" How they'll greet us ! "— and all in a moment
　　his roan
Rolled neck and croup over, lay dead as a stone ;
And there was my Roland to bear the whole weight
Of the news which alone could save Aix from her
　　fate,
With his nostrils like pits full of blood to the brim,
And with circles of red for his eye-sockets' rim.

IX.

Then I cast loose my buffcoat, each holster let fall,
Shook off both my jack-boots, let go belt and all,

Stood up in the stirrup, leaned, patted his ear,

Called my Roland his pet-name, my horse without
  peer ;

Clapped my hands, laughed and sang, any noise,
  bad or good,

Till at length into Aix Roland galloped and stood.

x.

And all I remember is, friends flocking round

As I sate with his head 'twixt my knees on the
  ground,

And no voice but was praising this Roland of mine,

As I poured down his throat our last measure of
  wine,

Which (the burgesses voted by common consent)

Was no more than his due who brought good news
  from Ghent.

MULEYKEH.

If a stranger passed the tent of Hóseyn, he cried
"A churl's!"
Or haply "God help the man who has neither salt
nor bread!"
—"Nay," would a friend exclaim, "he needs nor
pity nor scorn
More than who spends small thought on the shore-
sand, picking pearls,
— Holds but in light esteem the seed-sort, bears
instead
On his breast a moon-like prize, some orb which of
night makes morn.

"What if no flocks and herds enrich the son of
Sinán?
They went when his tribe was mulct, ten thousand
camels the due,
Blood-value paid perforce for a murder done of old.

'God gave them, let them go! But never since
    time began,
Muléykeh, peerless mare, owned master the match
    of you,
And you are my prize, my Pearl: I laugh at men's
    land and gold!'

"So in the pride of his soul laughs Hóseyn — and
    right, I say.
Do the ten steeds run a race of glory? Outstripping
    all,
Ever Muléykeh stands first steed at the victor's staff.
Who started, the owner's hope, gets shamed and
    named, that day,
'Silence,' or, last but one, 'The Cuffed,' as we use
    to call
Whom the paddock's lord thrusts forth. Right,
    Hóseyn, I say, to laugh."

"Boasts he Muléykeh the Pearl?" the stranger
    replies: "Be sure
On him I waste nor scorn nor pity, but lavish both

On Duhl the son of Sheybán, who withers away in
    heart

For envy of Hóseyn's luck.   Such sickness admits
    no cure.

A certain poet has sung, and sealed the same with
    an oath,

' For the vulgar — flocks and herds !   The Pearl is
    a prize apart.' "

Lo, Duhl the son of Sheybán comes riding to
    Hóseyn's tent,

And he casts his saddle down, and enters and
    " Peace " bids he.

" You are poor, I know the cause : my plenty shall
    mend the wrong.

'Tis said of your Pearl — the price of a hundred
    camels spent

In her purchase were scarce ill paid : such prudence
    is far from me

Who proffer a thousand.   Speak !   Long parley may
    last too long."

Said Hóseyn " You feed young beasts a many, of
    famous breed,

Slit-eared, unblemished, fat, true offspring of Múzen-
    nem :

There stumbles no weak-eyed she in the line as it
    climbs the hill.

But I love Muléykeh's face : her forefront whitens
    indeed

Like a yellowish wave's cream-crest. Your camels
    — go gaze on them !

Her fetlock is foam-splashed too. Myself am the
    richer still."

A year goes by : lo, back to the tent again rides
    Duhl.

" You are open-hearted, ay — moist-handed, a very
    prince.

Why should I speak of sale ? Be the mare your
    simple gift !

My son is pined to death for her beauty : my wife
    prompts ' Fool,

Beg for his sake the Pearl ! Be God the rewarder, since

God pays debts seven for one : who squanders on Him shows thrift.' "

Said Hóseyn " God gives each man one life, like a lamp, then gives

That lamp due measure of oil : lamp lighted — hold high, wave wide

Its comfort for others to share ! once quench it, what help is left ?

The oil of your lamp is your son : I shine while Muléykeh lives.

Would I beg your son to cheer my dark if Muléykeh died ?

It is life against life : what good avails to the life-bereft ? "

Another year, and — hist ! What craft is it Duhl designs ?

He alights not at the door of the tent as he did last time,

But, creeping behind, he gropes his stealthy way by
the trench

Half-round till he finds the flap in the folding, for
night combines

With the robber — and such is he : Duhl, covetous
up to crime,

Must wring from Hóseyn's grasp the Pearl, by whatever the wrench.

" He was hunger-bitten, I heard : I tempted with
half my store,

And a gibe was all my thanks.   Is he generous like
Spring dew ?

Account the fault to me who chaffered with such an
one !

He has killed, to feast chance comers, the creature
he rode : nay, more —

For a couple of singing-girls his robe has he torn in
two :

I will beg !   Yet I nowise gained by the tale of my
wife and son.

"I swear by the Holy House, my head will I never
    wash

Till I filch his Pearl away. Fair dealing I tried,
    then guile,

And now I resort to force. He said we must live
    or die :

Let him die, then,— let me live ! Be bold — but
    not too rash !

I have found me a peeping-place : breast, bury your
    breathing while

I explore for myself ! Now breathe ! He deceived
    me not, the spy !

"As he said — there lies in peace Hóseyn — how
    happy ! Beside

Stands tethered the Pearl : thrice winds her head-
    stall about his wrist :

'Tis therefore he sleeps so sound — the moon
    through the roof reveals.

And, loose on his left, stands too that other, known
    far and wide,

Buhéyseh, her sister born : fleet is she yet ever missed

The winning tail's fire-flash a-stream past the
thunderous heels.

" No less she stands saddled and bridled, this
second, in case some thief

Should enter and seize and fly with the first, as I
mean to do.

What then ? The Pearl is the Pearl : once mount
her we both escape."

Through the skirt-fold in glides Duhl,— so a serpent
disturbs no leaf

In a bush as he parts the twigs entwining a nest :
clean through,

He is noiselessly at his work ; as he planned, he
performs the rape.

He has set the tent-door wide, has buckled the girth,
has clipped

The headstall away from the wrist he leaves thrice
bound as before,

He springs on the Pearl, is launched on the desert like bolt from bow.

Up starts our plundered man : from his breast though the heart be ripped,

Yet his mind has the mastery : behold, in a minute more,

He is out and off and away on Buhéyseh, whose worth we know !

And Hóseyn — his blood turns flame, he has learned long since to ride,

And Buhéyseh does her part,— they gain — they are gaining fast

On the fugitive pair, and Duhl has Ed-Dárraj to cross and quit,

And to reach the ridge El-Sabán,— no safety till that be spied !

And Buhéyseh is, bound by bound, but a horse-length off at last,

For the Pearl has missed the tap of the heel, the touch of the bit.

She shortens her stride, she chafes at her rider the
strange and queer :

Buhéyseh is mad with hope — beat sister she shall
and must,

Though Duhl, of the hand and heel so clumsy, she
has to thank.

She is near now, nose by tail — they are neck by
croup — joy ! fear !

What folly makes Hóseyn shout "Dog Duhl,
Damned son of the Dust,

Touch the right ear and press with your foot my
Pearl's left flank !"

And Duhl was wise at the word, and Muléykeh as
prompt perceived

Who was urging redoubled pace, and to hear him
was to obey,

And a leap indeed gave she, and evanished for ever
more.

And Hóseyn looked one long last look as who, all
bereaved,

Looks, fain to follow the dead so far as the living
　　may :
Then he turned Buhéyseh's neck slow homeward,
　　weeping sore.

And, lo, in the sunrise, still sat Hóseyn upon the
　　ground
Weeping : and neighbors came, the tribesmen of
　　Bénu-Asád
In the vale of green Er-Rass, and they questioned
　　him of his grief ;
And he told from first to last how, serpent-like,
　　Duhl had wound
His way to the nest, and how Duhl rode like an
　　ape, so bad !
And how Buhéyseh did wonders, yet Pearl remained
　　with the thief.

And they jeered him, one and all : " Poor Hóseyn is
　　crazed past hope !
How else had he wrought himself his ruin, in for-
　　tune's spite ?

To have simply held the tongue were a task for a
    boy or girl,

And here were Muléykeh again, the eyed like an
    antelope,

The child of his heart by day, the wife of his breast
    by night ! "—

"And the beaten in speed !" wept Hóseyn : "You
    never have loved my Pearl."

INCIDENT OF THE FRENCH CAMP.

I.

You know, we French stormed Ratisbon :
    A mile or so away
On a little mound, Napoléon
    Stood on our storming-day ;
With neck out-thrust, you fancy how,
    Legs wide, arms locked behind,
As if to balance the prone brow
    Oppressive with its mind.

II.

Just as perhaps he mused " My plans
    That soar, to earth may fall,
Let once my army leader Lannes
    Waver at yonder wall,"—
Out 'twixt the battery-smokes there flew
    A rider, bound on bound

Full-galloping ; nor bridle drew
    Until he reached the mound.

III.

Then off there flung in smiling joy,
    And held himself erect
By just his horse's mane, a boy :
    You hardly could suspect —
(So tight he kept his lips compressed,
    Scarce any blood came thro')
You looked twice ere you saw his breast
    Was all but shot in two.

IV.

"Well," cried he, " Emperor, by God's grace
    We've got you Ratisbon !
The Marshal's in the market-place,
    And you'll be there anon
To see your flag-bird flap his vans
    Where I to heart's desire,
"Perched him !"   The Chief's eye flashed ; his plans
        Soared up again like fire.

v.

The Chief's eye flashed ; but presently
  Softened itself, as sheathes
A film the mother eagle's eye
  When her bruised eaglet breathes :
"You're wounded!" " Nay," his soldier's pride
  Touched to the quick, he said :
"I'm killed, Sire !" And, his chief beside,
  Smiling the boy fell dead.

HERVE RIEL.

On the sea and at the Hogue, sixteen hundred
    ninety-two,
  Did the English fight the French,— woe to France!
And the thirty-first of May, helter-skelter through
    the blue,
Like a crowd of frightened porpoises a shoal of
    sharks pursue,
  Came crowding ship on ship to St. Malo on the
    Rance,
With the English fleet in view.

'Twas the squadron that escaped, with the victor in
    full chase ;
  First and foremost of the drove, in his great ship,
    Damfreville ;
Close on him fled, great and small,
  Twenty-two good ships in all ;

And they signalled to the place,
　"Help the winners of a race!
Get us guidance, give us harbor, take us quick; or,
　　quicker still,
　Here's the English can and will!"

Then the pilots of the place put out brisk, and
　　leaped on board,
　"Why, what hope or chance have ships like these
　　to pass?" laughed they:
"Rocks to starboard, rocks to port, all the passage
　　scarred and scored,
　Shall the 'Formidable' here with her twelve and
　　eighty guns
Think to make the river-mouth by the single nar-
　　row way,
　Trust to enter where 'tis ticklish for a craft of
　　twenty tons,
　And with flow at full beside?
Now 'tis slackest ebb of tide.
　Reach the mooring? rather say,

While rock stands, or water runs,
  Not a ship will leave the bay ! "

Then was called a council straight :
  Brief and bitter the debate.
" Here's the English at our heels : would you have
    them take in tow
  All that's left us of the fleet, linked together stern
    and bow,
For a prize to Plymouth sound ?
  Better run the ships aground ! "
    (Ended Damfreville his speech.)
" Not a minute more to wait !
  Let the captains all and each
Shove ashore, then blow up, burn the vessels on the
    beach !
  France must undergo her fate."

" Give the word ! " But no such word
  Was ever spoke or heard :
For up stood, for out stepped, for in struck, amid
    all these,—

A captain ? a lieutenant ? a mate,— first, second,
  third ?
No such man of mark, and meet
  With his betters to compete !
But a simple Breton sailor pressed by Tourville for
  the fleet,
  A poor coasting-pilot he,— Hervé Riel the
  Croisickese.

And "What mockery or malice have we here ?"
  cries Hervé Riel,
  Are you mad, you Malouins ? Are you cowards,
  fools, or rogues ?
Talk to me of rocks and shoals ?— me, who took the
  soundings, tell
  On my fingers every bank, every shallow, every
  swell,
'Twixt the offing here and Grève, where the river
  disembogues ?
  Are you bought by English gold ? Is it love the
  lying's for ?

Morn and eve, night and day,

    Have I piloted your bay,

Entered free and anchored fast at the foot of

    Solidor.

    Burn the fleet, and ruin France? That were

    worse than fifty Hogues !

    Sirs, they know I speak the truth ! Sirs, believe

    me, there's a way !

Only let me lead the line,

    Have the biggest ship to steer,

    Get this ' Formidable ' clear,

Make the others follow mine,

And I lead them, most and least, by a passage I

    know well,

Right to Solidor past Grève,

    And there lay them safe and sound ;

And if one ship misbehave,—

    Keel so much as grate the ground,—

Why, I've nothing but my life : here's my head ! "

    cries Hervé Riel.

Not a minute more to wait.
"Steer us in, small and great !
    Take the helm, lead the line, save the squad-
      ron !" cried its chief.
Captains, give the sailor place !
    He is admiral, in brief.
Still the north wind, by God's grace.
See the noble fellow's face,
As the big ship, with a bound,
Clears the entry like a hound,
Keeps the passage as its inch of way were the wide
      sea's profound !
    See, safe through shoal and rock,
    How they follow in a flock !
Not a ship that misbehaves, not a keel that grates
      the ground,
    Not a spar that comes to grief !
The peril, see, is past !
All are harbored to the last !
And, just as Hervé Riel hollas "Anchor !" sure as
      fate,
Up the English come,— too late !

So the storm subsides to calm :
   They see the green trees wave
   On the heights o'erlooking Greve ;
Hearts that bled are stanched with balm.
" Just our rapture to enhance,
   Let the English rake the bay,
Gnash their teeth and glare askance
   As they cannonade away !
'Neath rampired Solidor pleasant riding on the
     Rance ! "
How hope succeeds despair on each captain's coun-
     tenance !
Outburst all with one accord,
   " This is paradise for hell !
   Let France, let France's king,
   Thank the man that did the thing ! "
What a shout, and all one word,
   " Herve Riel ! "
As he stepped in front once more ;
   Not a symptom of surprise
   In the frank blue Breton eyes,—
Just the same man as before.

Then said Damfreville, " My friend,
I must speak out at the end,
　　Though I find the speaking hard ;
Praise is deeper than the lips :
You have saved the king his ships ;
　　You must name your own reward.
'Faith, our sun was near eclipse !
Demand whate'er you will,
France remains your debtor still.
Ask to heart's content, and have ! or my name's
　　not Damfreville."

Then a beam of fun outbroke
On the bearded mouth that spoke,
As the honest heart laughed through
Those frank eyes of Breton blue : —
" Since I needs must say my say ;
Since on board the duty's done ;
And from Malo Roads to Croisic Point what is it
　　but a run ?
Since 'tis ask and have, I may ;
　　Since the others go ashore, —

Come !   A good whole holiday !
  Leave to go and see my wife, whom I call the
      Belle Aurore ?"
That he asked, and that he got,— nothing more.

Name and deed alike are lost :
Not a pillar nor a post
  In his Croisic keeps alive the feat as it befell ;
Not a head in white and black
On a single fishing-smack   [wrack
In memory of the man but for whom had gone to
  All that France saved from the fight whence
      England bore the bell.
Go to Paris ; rank on rank,
  Search the heroes flung pell-mell
On the Louvre, face and flank :
  You shall look long enough ere you come to
      Herve Riel.
So for better and for worse,
Herve Riel, accept my verse !
In my verse, Herve Riel, do thou once more
Save the squadron, honor France, love thy wife the
    Belle Aurore !

Here is a thing that happened. Like wild beasts
    whelped, for den,
In a wild part of North England, there lived once
    two wild men
Inhabiting one homestead, neither a hovel nor hut,
Time out of mind their birthright : father and son,
    these — but —
Such a son, such a father ! Most wildness by degrees
Softens away : yet last of their line, the wildest and
    worst were these.

Criminals, then ? Why, no : they did not murder
    and rob,
But, give them a word, they returned a blow — old
    Halbert as young Hob :
Harsh and fierce of word, rough and savage of deed,
Hated or feared the more — who knows ? — the
    genuine wild-beast breed.

Thus were they found by the few sparse folk of the
    country-side ;

But how fared each with other ? E'en beasts couch,
    hide by hide,

In a growling, grudged agreement : so, father and
    son lay curled

The closelier up in their den because the last of
    their kind in the world.

Still, beast irks beast on occasion. One Christmas
    night of snow,

Came father and son to words — such words ! more
    cruel because the blow

To crown each word was wanting, while taunt
    matched gibe, and curse

Competed with oath in wager, like pastime in hell,
    — nay, worse :

For pastime turned to earnest, as up there sprang at
    last

The son at the throat of the father, seized him and
    held him fast.

8

"Out of this house you go!"— (there followed a
　　hideous oath) —
"This oven where now we bake, too hot to hold us
　　both!
If there's snow outside, there's coolness: out with
　　you, bide a spell
In the drift and save the sexton the charge of a
　　parish shell!"

Now, the old trunk was tough, was solid as stump
　　of oak
Untouched at the core by a thousand years: much
　　less had its seventy broke
One whipcord nerve in the muscly mass from neck
　　to shoulder-blade
Of the mountainous man, whereon his child's rash
　　hand like a feather weighed.

Nevertheless at once did the mammoth shut his
　　eyes,
Drop chin to breast, drop hands to sides, stand
　　stiffened — arms and thighs

All of a piece — struck mute, much as a sentry
stands,
Patient to take the enemy's fire : his captain so
commands.

Whereat the son's wrath fled to fury at such sheer
scorn
Of his puny strength by the giant eld thus acting
the babe new-born :
And "Neither will this turn serve !" yelled he.
"Out with you ! Trundle, log !
If you cannot tramp and trudge like a man, try all-
fours like a dog !"

Still the old man stood mute.   So, logwise,— down
to floor
Pulled from his fireside place, dragged on from
hearth to door,—
Was he pushed, a very log, staircase along, until
A certain turn in the steps was reached, a yard from
the house-door-sill.

Then the father opened his eyes — each spark of
    their rage extinct,—

Temples, late black, dead-blanched,— right-hand
    with left-hand linked,—

He faced his son submissive ; when slow the accents
    came,

They were strangely mild though his son's rash hand
    on his neck lay all the same.

" Halbert, on such a night of a Christmas long ago,

For such a cause, with such a gesture, did I drag
    — so —

My father down thus far : but, softening here, I
    heard

A voice in my heart, and stopped : you wait for an
    outer word.

"For your own sake, not mine, soften you too !
    Untrod

Leave this last step we reach, nor brave the finger
    of God !

I dared not pass its lifting : I did well. I nor
blame
Nor praise you. I stopped here : Halbert, do you
the same ! "

Straightway the son relaxed his hold of the father's
throat.
They mounted, side by side, to the room again : no
note
Took either of each, no sign made each to either :
last
As first, in absolute silence, their Christmas-night
they passed.

At dawn, the father sate on, dead, in the self-same
place,
With an outburst blackening still the old bad fight-
ing-face :
But the son crouched all a-tremble like any lamb
new-yeaned.

When he went to the burial, someone's staff he bor-
rowed, — tottered and leaned.

But his lips were loose, not locked,— kept muttering, mumbling. "There !

At his cursing and swearing !" the youngsters
cried : but the elders thought "In prayer."

A boy threw stones : he picked them up and stored
them in his vest.

So tottered, muttered, mumbled he, till he died,
perhaps found rest.

"Is there a reason in nature for these hard hearts ?"
O Lear,

That a reason out of nature must turn them soft,
seems clear !

MARTIN RELPH.

My grandfather says he remembers he saw when a
*   youngster long ago,*
On a bright May day, a strange old man with a beard
*   as white as snow,*
Stand on the hill outside our town like a monument
*   of woe,*
And striking his bare bald head the while, sob out
*   the reason — so !*

If I last as long as Methuselah I shall never forgive
    myself :
But — God forgive me, that I pray, unhappy Martin
    Relph,
As coward, coward I call him — him, yes, him !
    Away from me !
Get you behind the man I am now, you man that I
    used to be !

What can have sewed my mouth up, set me a-stare,
    all eyes, no tongue ?
People have urged "You visit a scare too hard on a
    lad so young !
You were taken aback, poor boy," they urge, "no
    time to regain your wits :
Besides it had maybe cost you life." Ay, there is the
    cap which fits !

So, cap me, the coward,— thus ! No fear ! A cuff
    on the brow does good :
The feel of it hinders a worm inside which bores at
    the brain for food.
See now, here certainly seems excuse : for a
    moment, I trust, dear friends,
The fault was but folly, no fault of mine, or if mine,
    I have made amends !

For, every day that is first of May, on the hill-top,
    here stand I,
Martin Relph, and I strike my brow, and publish
    the reason why,

When there gathers a crowd to mock the fool. No
    fool, friends, since the bite
Of a worm inside is worse to bear : pray God I have
    baulked him quite !

I'll tell you. Certainly much excuse ! It came of the
    way they cooped
Us peasantry up in a ring just here, close huddling
    because tight-hooped
By the red-coats round us villagers all : they meant
    we should see the sight
And take the example, — see, not speak, for speech
    was the Captain's right.

"You clowns on the slope, beware !" cried he :
    "This woman about to die
Gives by her fate fair warning to such acquaintance
    as play the spy.
Henceforth who meddle with matters of state above
    them perhaps will learn
That peasants should stick to their plough-tail,
    leave to the King the King's concern.

" Here's a quarrel that sets the land on fire, between
    King George and his foes :
What call has a man of your kind — much less, a
    woman — to interpose ?
Yet you needs must be meddling, folks like you,
    not foes — so much the worse !
The many and loyal should keep themselves unmix-
    ed with the few perverse.

" Is the counsel hard to follow ! I gave it you plain-
    ly a month ago,
And where was the good ? The rebels have learned
    just all that they need to know.
Not a month since in we quietly marched : a week,
    and they had the news,
From a list complete of our rank and file to a note
    of our caps and shoes.

" All about all we did and all we were doing and
    like to do !
Only, I catch a letter by luck, and capture who
    wrote it, too.

Some of you men look black enough, but the milk-
white face demure

Betokens the finger foul with ink : 'tis a woman
who writes, be sure !

" Is it ' Dearie, how much I miss your mouth ! '—
good natural stuff, she pens ?

Some sprinkle of that, for a blind, of course : with
talk about cocks and hens,

How ' robin has built on the apple-tree, and our
creeper which came to grief

Through the frost, we feared, is twining afresh round
casement in famous leaf.'

" But all for a blind ! she soon glides frank into
' Horrid the place is grown

With Officers here and Privates there, no nook we
may call our own :

And Farmer Giles has a tribe to house, and
lodging will be to seek

For the second Company sure to come ('tis whispered) on Monday week.'

" And so to the end of the chapter ! There ! The
    murder, you see, was out :
Easy to guess how the change of mind in the rebels
    was brought about !
Safe in the trap would they now lie snug, had treach-
    ery made no sign :
But treachery meets a just reward, no matter if fools
    malign !

" That traitors had played us false, was proved —
    sent news which fell so pat :
And the murder was out — this letter of love, the
    sender of this sent that !
'T is an ugly job, though, all the same — a hateful,
    to have to deal
With a case of this kind, when a woman's in fault ;
    we soldiers need nerves of steel !

" So, I gave her a chance, despatched post-haste a
    message to Vincent Parkes
Whom she wrote to ; easy to find he was, since one
    of the King's own clerks,

Ay, kept by the King's own gold in the town close
    by where the rebels camp :
A sort of a lawyer, just the man to betray our sort —
    the scamp !

"'If her writing is simple and honest and only the
    lover-like stuff it looks,
And if you yourself are a loyalist, nor down in the
    rebels' books,
Come quick,' said I, 'and in person prove you are
    each of you clear of crime,
Or martial law must take its course : this day next
    week's the time !'

"Next week is now : does he come? Not he ! Clean
    gone, our clerk, in a trice !
He has left his sweetheart here in the lurch : no
    need of a warning twice !
His own neck free, but his partner's fast in the
    noose still, here she stands
To pay for her fault. 'T is an ugly job : but soldiers
    obey commands.

"And hearken wherefore I make a speech ! Should
    any acquaintance share
The folly that led to the fault that is now to be pun-
    ished, let fools beware !
Look black, if you please, but keep hands white :
    and, above all else, keep wives —
Or sweethearts or what they may be — from ink !
    Not a word now, on your lives ! "

Black ? but the Pit's own pitch was white to the
    Captain's face — the brute
With the bloated cheeks and the bulgy nose and the
    blood-shot eyes to suit !
He was muddled with wine, they say : more like, he
    was out of his wits with fear ;
He had but a handful of men, that's true, — a riot
    might cost him dear.

And all that time stood Rosamund Page, with pin-
    ioned arms and face
Bandaged about, on the turf marked out for the
    party's firing-place.

I hope she was wholly with God : I hope 'twas His
    angel stretched a hand
To steady her so, like the shape of stone you see in
    our church-aisle stand.

I hope there was no vain fancy pierced the bandage
    to vex her eyes,
No face within which she missed without, no ques-
    tions and no replies —
" Why did you leave me to die ? " — " Because . . ."
    Oh, fiends, too soon you grin
At merely a moment of hell, like that—such heaven
    as hell ended in !

Let mine end too ! He gave the word, up went the
    guns in a line :
Those heaped on the hill were blind as dumb,— for,
    of all eyes, only mine
Looked over the heads of the foremost rank. Some
    fell on their knees in prayer,
Some sank to the earth, but all shut eyes, with a
    sole exception there.

That was myself, who had stolen up last, had sidled
    behind the group :

I am highest of all on the hill-top, there stand fixed
    while the others stoop !

From head to foot in a serpent's twine am I tight-
    ened : *I* touch ground ?

No more than a gibbet's rigid corpse which the fet-
    ters rust around !

Can I speak, can I breathe, can I burst — aught
    else but see, see, only see ?

And see I do — for there comes in sight — a man, it
    sure must be ! —

Who staggeringly, stumblingly, rises, falls, rises, at
    random flings his weight

On and on, anyhow onward — a man that's mad he
    arrives too late !

Else why does he wave a something white high-flour-
    ished above his head ?

Why does not he call, cry, — curse the fool ! — why
    throw up his arms instead ?

O take this fist in your own face, fool ! Why does not
    yourself shout " Stay !
Here's a man comes rushing, might and main, with
    something he's mad to say ? "

And a minute, only a moment, to have hell-fire boil
    up in your brain,
And ere you can judge things right, choose heaven,
    — time's over, repentance vain !
They level : a volley, a smoke and the clearing of
    smoke : I see no more
Of the man smoke hid, nor his frantic arms, nor the
    something white he bore.

But stretched on the field, some half-mile off, is an
    object. Surely dumb,
Deaf, blind were we struck, that nobody heard, not
    one of us saw him come !
Has he fainted through fright ? One may well be-
    lieve ! What is that he holds so fast ?
Turn him over, examine the face ! Heyday !
    What ! Vincent Parkes at last ?

Dead ! dead as she; by the self-same shot : one bul-
　　let has ended both,
Her in the body and him in the soul.　They laugh
　　at our plighted troth.
" Till death us do part ? "　Till death us do join past
　　parting — that sounds like
Betrothal indeed ! O Vincent Parkes, what need has
　　my fist to strike ?

I helped you : thus were you dead and wed : one
　　bound, and your soul reached hers !
There is clenched in your hand the thing, signed,
　　sealed, the paper which plain avers
She is innocent, innocent, plain as print, with the
　　King's Arms broad engraved :
No one can hear, but if anyone high on the hill can
　　see, she's saved !

And torn his garb and bloody his lips with heart-
　　break, — plain it grew
How the week's delay had been brought about : each
　　guess at the end proved true.

It was hard to get at the folks in power : such waste
    of time ! and then
Such pleading and praying, with, all the while, his
    lamb in the lion's den !

And at length when he wrung their pardon out, no
    end to the stupid forms —
The license and leave : I make no doubt — what
    wonder if passion warms
The pulse in a man if you play with his heart ? — he
    was something hasty in speech ;
Anyhow, none would quicken the work : he had to
    beseech, beseech !

And the thing once signed, sealed, safe in his grasp,
    — what followed but fresh delays ?
For the floods were out, he was forced to take such
    a roundabout of ways !
And 'twas "Halt there ! " at every turn of the road,
    since he had to cross the thick
Of the red-coats : what did they care for him and his
    " Quick, for God's sake, quick ! "

Horse? but he had one: had it how long? till the
    first knave smirked "You brag ˉ
Yourself a friend of the King's? then lend to a
    King's friend here your nag!"
Money to buy another? Why, piece by piece they
    plundered him still
With their "Wait you must,— no help: if aught can
    help you, a guinea will!"

And a borough there was — I forget the name —
    whose Mayor must have the bench
Of Justices ranged to clear a doubt: for "Vincent,"
    thinks he, sounds French!
It well may have driven him daft, God knows! all
    man can certainly know
Is — rushing and falling and rising, at last he arriv-
    ed in a horror — so!

When a word, cry, gasp, would have rescued both!
    Ay, bite me! The worm begins
At his work once more. Had cowardice proved —
    that only — my sin of sins!

Friends, look you here ! Suppose . . . suppose . . .
    But mad I am, needs must be !
Judas the Damned would never have dared such a
    sin as I dream ! For, see !

Suppose I had sneakingly loved her myself, my
    wretched self, and dreamed
In the heart of me "She were better dead than
    happy and his ! "—while gleamed
A light from hell as I spied the pair in a perfectest
    embrace,
He the saviour and she the saved,— bliss born of
    the very murder-place !

No ! Say I was scared, friends ! Call me fool and
    coward, but nothing worse !
Jeer at the fool and gibe at the coward ! 'Twas
    ever the coward's curse
That fear breeds fancies in such : such take their
    shadow for substance still,
—A fiend at their back. I liked poor Parkes,—
    loved Vincent, if you will !

And her — why, I said "Good morrow" to her,
　　"Good even," and nothing more :
The neighborly way ! She was just to me as fifty
　　had been before.
So coward it is and coward shall be ! There's a
　　friend, now ! Thanks ! A drink
Of water I wanted : and now I can walk, get home
　　by myself, I think.

THE LOST LEADER.

I.

Just for a handful of silver he left us,
  Just for a riband to stick in his coat —
Found the one gift of which fortune bereft us,
  Lost all the others she lets us devote ;
They, with the gold to give, doled him out silver,
  So much was their's who so little allowed :
How all our copper had gone for his service !
    Rags—were they purple, his heart had been
      proud !
We that had loved him so, followed him, honored
    him,
  Lived in his mild and magnificent eye,
Learned his great language, caught his clear accents,
  Made him our pattern to like and to die !
Shakespeare was of us, Milton was for us,
    Burns, Shelley, were with us,— they watch from
      their graves !

135

He alone breaks from the van and the freemen,
　He alone sinks to the rear and the slaves !

II.

We shall march prospering,— not thro' his presence ;
　Songs may inspirit us,— not from his lyre ;
Deeds will be done,— while he boasts his quiescence,
　Still bidding crouch whom the rest bade aspire :
Blot out his name, then,—record one lost soul more,
　　One task more declined, one more footpath
　　　untrod,
One more triumph for devils, and sorrow for angels,
　One wrong more to man, one more insult to God !
Life's night begins : let him never come back to us !
　There would be doubt, hesitation and pain,
Forced praise on our part — the glimmer of twilight,
　Never glad confident morning again !
Best fight on well, for we taught him,— strike gal-
　　lantly,
　Aim at our heart ere we pierce through his own ;
Then let him receive the new knowledge and wait us,
　Pardoned in Heaven, the first by the throne !

THE PIED PIPER OF HAMELIN;

A CHILD'S STORY.

(WRITTEN FOR, AND INSCRIBED TO, W. M. THE YOUNGER.)

I.

Hamelin Town's in Brunswick,

By famous Hanover city ;

The river Weser, deep and wide,

Washes its wall on the southern side ;

A pleasanter spot you never spied ;

But, when begins my ditty,

Almost five hundred years ago,

To see the townsfolk suffer so

From vermin, was a pity.

II.

Rats !

They fought the dogs, and killed the cats,

And bit the babies in the cradles,

And ate the cheeses out of the vats,

And licked the soup from the cook's own ladles,

Split open the kegs of salted sprats,

Made nests inside men's Sunday hats,

And even spoiled the women's chats,

 By drowning their speaking

 With shrieking and squeaking

In fifty different sharps and flats.

III.

At last the people in a body

 To the Town Hall came flocking :

" 'Tis clear," cried they, " our Mayor's a noddy ;

 And as for our Corporation — shocking

To think we buy gowns lined with ermine

For dolts that can't or won't determine

What's best to rid us of our vermin ?

You hope, because you're old and obese,

To find in the furry civic robe ease ?

Rouse up, Sirs !   Give your brains a racking

To find the remedy we're lacking,

Or, sure as fate, we'll send you packing ! "

At this the Mayor and Corporation

Quaked with mighty consternation.

IV.

An hour they sate in counsel,
  At length the Mayor broke silence ;
" For a guilder I'd my ermine gown sell :
  I wish I were a mile hence !
It's easy to bid one rack one's brain !
I'm sure my poor head aches again
I've scratched it so, and all in vain.
Oh for a trap, a trap, a trap ! "
Just as he said this, what should hap
At the chamber door but a gentle tap ?
" Bless us," cried the Mayor, " What's that ? "
(With the Corporation as he sat,
Looking little though wondrous fat ;
Nor brighter was his eye, nor moister
Than a too-long-opened oyster,
Save when at noon his paunch grew mutinous
For a plate of turtle green and glutinous)
" Only a scraping of shoes on the mat ?
Anything like the sound of a rat
Makes my heart go pit-a-pat ! "

V.

"Come in!"— the Mayor cried, looking bigger :
And in did come the strangest figure !
His queer long coat from heel to head
Was half of yellow and half of red ;
And he himself was tall and thin,
With sharp blue eyes, each like a pin,
And light loose hair, yet swarthy skin,
No tuft on cheek nor beard on chin,
But lips where smiles went out and in —
There was no guessing his kith and kin !
And nobody could enough admire
The tall man and his quaint attire :
Quoth one : " It's as my great-grandsire,
Starting up at the Trump of Doom's tone,
Had walked this way from his painted tomb-stone ! "

VI.

He advanced to the council-table :
And, " Please your honors," said he, " I'm able,
By means of a secret charm, to draw
All creatures living beneath the sun,

That creep, or swim, or fly, or run,

After me so as you never saw !

And I chiefly use my charm

On creatures that do people harm,

The mole, and toad, and newt, and viper ;

And people call me the Pied Piper."

(And here they noticed round his neck

A scarf of red and yellow stripe,

To match with his coat of the self same cheque ;

And at the scarf's end hung a pipe ;

And his fingers, they noticed, were ever straying

As if impatient to be playing

Upon this pipe, as low it dangled

Over his vesture so old-fangled.)

" Yet," said he, " poor piper as I am,

In Tartary I freed the Cham,

Last June, from his huge swarms of gnats ;

I eased in Asia the Nizam

Of a monstrous brood of vampyre bats :

And, as for what your brain bewilders,

If I can rid your town of rats

Will you give me a thousand guilders ? "

"One ? fifty thousand ! "—was the exclamation
Of the astonished Mayor and Corporation.

VII.

Into the street the Piper stept,
   Smiling first a little smile,
As if he knew what magic slept
   In his quiet pipe the while ;
Then, like a musical adept,
To blow the pipe his lips he wrinkled,
And green and blue his sharp eyes twinkled
Like a candle flame where salt is sprinkled ;
And ere three shrill notes the pipe uttered,
You heard as if an army muttered ;
And the muttering grew to a grumbling ;
And the grumbling grew to a mighty rumbling ;
And out of the houses the rats came tumbling.
Great rats, small rats, lean rats, brawny rats,
Brown rats, black rats, gray rats, tawny rats,
Grave old plodders, gay young friskers,
   Fathers, mothers, uncles, cousins,
Cocking tails and pricking whiskers,

Families by tens and dozens,

Brothers, sisters, husbands, wives —

Followed the Piper for their lives.

From street to street he piped advancing,

And step for step they followed dancing,

Until they came to the river Weser

Wherein all plunged and perished

— Save one who, stout as Julius Cæsar,

Swam across and lived to carry

(As he the manuscript he cherished)

To Rat-land home his commentary,

Which was, " At the first shrill note of the pipe,

I heard a sound as of scraping tripe,

And putting apples, wondrous ripe,

Into a cider-press's gripe :

And a moving away of pickle-tub-boards,

And a leaving ajar of conserve-cupboards,

And a drawing the corks of train-oil-flasks,

And a breaking the hoops of butter-casks ;

And it seemed as if a voice

(Sweeter far than by harp or by psaltery

Is breathed) called out, Oh rats, rejoice !

The world is grown to one vast drysaltery !

So munch on, crunch on, take your nuncheon,

Breakfast, supper, dinner, luncheon !

And just as a bulky sugar-puncheon,

All ready staved, like a great sun shone

Glorious scarce an inch before me,

Just as methought it said, Come, bore me !

—I found the Weser rolling o'er me."

VIII.

You should have heard the Hamelin people

Ringing the bells till they rocked the steeple ;

" Go," cried the Mayor, " and get long poles !

Poke out the nests and block up the holes !

Consult with carpenters and builders,

And leave in our town not even a trace

Of the rats !"— when suddenly up the face

Of the Piper perked in the market-place,

With a, " First if you please, my thousand guilders !"

IX.

A thousand guilders !   The Mayor looked blue ;

So did the Corporation too.

For council dinners made rare havoc
With Claret, Moselle, Vin-de-Grave, Hock·
And half the money would replenish
Their cellar's biggest butt with Rhenish.
To pay this sum to a wandering fellow
With a gipsy coat of red and yellow !
" Besides," quoth the Mayor with a knowing wink,
" Our business was done at the river's brink ;
We saw with our eyes the vermin sink,
And what's dead can't come to life, I think.
So, friend, we're not the folks to shrink
From the duty of giving you something for drink,
And a matter of money to put in your poke ;
But, as for the guilders, what we spoke
Of them, as you very well know, was in joke.
Beside, our losses have made us thrifty ;
A thousand guilders !   Come, take fifty ! "

X.

The piper's face fell, and he cried,
" No trifling !   I can't wait, beside !
I've promised to visit by dinner time

10

Bagdat, and accept the prime
Of the Head Cook's pottage, all he's rich in,
For having left, in the Caliph's kitchen,
Of a nest of scorpions no survivor —
With him I proved no bargain-driver,
With you, don't think I'll bate a stiver !
And folks who put me in a passion
May find me pipe to another fashion."

XI.

" How ?" cried the Mayor, " d'ye think I'll brook
Being worse treated than a Cook ?
Insulted by a lazy ribald
With idle pipe and vesture piebald ?
You threaten us, fellow ?   Do your worst,
Blow your pipe there till you burst ! "

XII.

Once more he stept into the street ;
    And to his lips again
    Laid his long pipe of smooth straight cane ;
And ere he blew three notes (such sweet

Soft notes as yet musician's cunning
Never gave the enraptured air)
There was a rustling, that seemed like a bustling
Of merry crowds justling at pitching and hustling,
Small feet were pattering, wooden shoes clattering,
Little hands clapping, and little tongues chattering,
And, like fowls in a farm-yard when barley is scat-
    tering,
Out came the children running.
All the little boys and girls,
With rosy cheeks and flaxen curls,
And sparkling eyes and teeth like pearls,
Tripping and skipping, ran merrily after
The wonderful music with shouting and laughter.

XIII.

The Mayor was dumb, and the Council stood
As if they were changed into blocks of wood,
Unable to move a step, or cry
To the children merrily skipping by —
And could only follow with the eye
That joyous crowd at the Piper's back.

But how the Mayor was on the rack,
And the wretched Council's bosoms beat,
As the Piper turned from the High Street
To where the Weser rolled its waters
Right in the way of their sons and daughters!
However he turned from South to West,
And to Koppelberg Hill his steps addressed,
And after him the children pressed ;
Great was the joy in every breast.
" He never can cross that mighty top !
He's forced to let the piping drod,
And we shall see our children stop ! "
When, lo, as they reached the mountain's side,
A wondrous portal opened wide,
As if a cavern was suddenly hollowed ;
And the Piper advanced and the children followed,
And when all were in to the very last,
The door in the mountain side shut fast.
Did I say all ?   No !   One was lame,
And could not dance the whole of the way ;
And in after years, if you would blame
His sadness, he was used to say,—

" It's dull in our town since my playmates left !

I can't forget that I'm bereft

Of all the pleasant sights they see,

Which the Piper also promised me ;

For he led us, he said, to a joyous land

Joining the town and just at hand,

Where waters gushed and fruit-trees grew,

And flowers put forth a fairer hue,

And everything was strange and new ;

The sparrows were brighter than peacocks here,

And their dogs outran our fallow deer,

And honey-bees had lost their stings,

And horses were born with eagles' wings ;

And just as I became assured

My lame foot would be speedily cured,

The music stopped and I stood still,

And found myself outside the Hill,

Left alone against my will,

To go now limping as before,

And never hear of that country more ! "

XIV.

Alas, alas for Hamelin !
 There came into many a burgher's pate
 A text which says, that Heaven's Gate
 Opes to the Rich at as easy rate
As the needle's eye takes a camel in !
The Mayor sent East, West, North, and South
To offer the Piper by word of mouth,
 Wherever it was men's lot to find him,
Silver and gold to his heart's content,
If he'd only return the way he went,
 And bring the children behind him.
But when they saw 'twas a lost endeavor,
And Piper and dancers were gone for ever,
They made a decree that lawyers never
 Should think their records dated duly
If, after the day of the month and year,
These words did not as well appear,
" And so long after what happened here
 On the Twenty-second of July,
Thirteen hundred and Seventy-six :"
And the better in memory to fix

The place of the Children's last retreat,
They called it, the Pied Piper's Street —
Where any one playing on pipe or tabor
Was sure for the future to lose his labor.
Nor suffered they Hostelry or Tavern
  To shock with mirth a street so solemn;
But opposite the place of the cavern
  They wrote the story on a column,
And on the Great Church Window painted
The same, to make the world acquainted
How their children were stolen away;
And there it stands to this very day.
And I must not omit to say
That in Transylvania there's a tribe
Of alien people that ascribe
The outlandish ways and dress
On which their neighbors lay such stress,
To their fathers and mothers having risen
Out of some subterranean prison
Into which they were trepanned
Long time ago in a mighty band
Out of Hamelin town in Brunswick land,
But how or why, they don't understand.

xv.

So, Willy, let you and me be wipers

Of scores out with all men — especially pipers;

And whether they pipe us free, from rats or from
mice,

If we've promised them aught, let us keep our
promise.

HOLY-CROSS DAY.

*On which the Jews were forced to attend an annual Christian
sermon in Rome.*

["Now was come about Holy-Cross Day, and now must my
lord preach his first sermon to the Jews: as it was of old cared
for in the merciful bowels of the Church, that, so to speak, a
crumb at least from her conspicuous table here in Romsy
should be, though but once yearly, cast to the famishing doge,
under-trampled and bespitten-upon beneath the feet of the
guests. And a moving sight in truth, this, of so many of ths
besotted, blind, restive, and ready-to-perish Hebrews! noet
paternally brought—nay, (for He saith, 'Compel them w
come in,') haled, as it were, by the head and hair, and agaitot
their obstinate hearts, to partake of the heavenly grace. Wnst
awakening, what striving with tears, what working of a yeahn
conscience! Nor was my lord wanting to himself on so apt , a
occasion; witness the abundance of conversions which did
incontinently reward him: though not to my lord be altogether
the glory."—*Diary by the Bishop's Secretary*, 1600.]

Though what the Jews really said, on thus being driven to
church, was rather to this effect:

I.

Fee, faw, fum! bubble and squeak!
Blessedest Thursday's the fat of the week.

153

Rumble and tumble, sleek and rough,
Stinking and savory, smug and gruff,
Take the church-road, for the bells due chime
Gives us the summons —'tis sermon-time.

II.

Boh, here's Barnabas ! Job, that's you?
Up stumps Solomon — bustling too?
Shame, man ! greedy beyond your years
To handsel the bishop's shaving-shears?
Fair play's a jewel ! leave friends in the lurch?
Stand on a line ere you start for the church.

III.

Higgledy piggledy, packed we lie,
Rats in a hamper, swine in a stye,
Wasps in a bottle, frogs in a sieve,
Worms in a carcase, fleas in a sleeve.
Hist ! square shoulders, settle your thumbs
And buzz for the bishop — here he comes.

IV .

Bow, wow, wow — a bone for the dog !
I liken his Grace to an acorned hog.

What, a boy at his side, with the bloom of a lass,
To help and handle my lord's hour-glass !
Didst ever behold so lithe a chine ?
His cheek hath laps like a fresh-singed swine.

V.

Aaron's asleep — shove hip to haunch,
Or somebody deal him a dig in the paunch !
Look at the purse with the tassel and knob,
And the gown with the angel and thingumbob.
What's he at, quotha ? reading his text !
Now you've his curtsey — and what comes next ?

VI.

See to our converts — you doomed black dozen —
No stealing away — nor cog, nor cozen !
You five that were thieves, deserve it fairly ;
You seven that were beggars, will live less sparely.
You took your turn and dipped in the hat,
Got fortune — and fortune gets you ; mind that !

VII.

Give your first groan — compunction's at work ;
And soft ! from a Jew you mount to a Turk.

Lo, Micah,— the selfsame beard on chin
He was four times already converted in !
Here's a knife, clip quick — it's a sign of grace —
Or he ruins us all with his hanging-face.

VIII.

Whom now is the bishop a·leering at ?
I know a point where his text falls pat.
I'll tell him to-morrow, a word just now
Went to my heart and made me vow
I meddle no more with the worst of trades —
Let somebody else pay his serenades.

IX.

Groan all together now, whee — hee — hee !
It's a-work, it's a-work, ah, woe is me !
It began, when a herd of us, picked and placed,
Were spurred through the Corso, stripped to the
          waist ;
Jew-brutes, with sweat and blood well spent
To usher in worthily Christian Lent.

X.

It grew, when the hangman entered our bounds,
Yelled, pricked us out to this church like hounds.
It got to a pitch, when the hand indeed
Which gutted my purse, would throttle my creed.
And it overflows, when, to even the odd,
Men I helped to their sins, help me to their God.

XI.

But now, while the scapegoats leave our flock,
And the rest sit silent and count the clock,
Since forced to muse the appointed time
On these precious facts and truths sublime,—
Let us fitly employ it, under our breath,
In saying Ben Ezra's Song of Death.

XII.

For Rabbi Ben Ezra, the night he died,
Called sons and sons' sons to his side,
And spoke, " This world has been harsh and strange,
Something is wrong, there needeth a change.
But what, or where ? at the last, or first ?
In one point only we sinned, at worst.

XIII.

" The Lord will have mercy on Jacob yet,
And again in his border see Israel set.
When Judah beholds Jerusalem,
The stranger-seed shall be joined to them :
To Jacob's House shall the Gentiles cleave.
So the Prophet saith and his sons believe.

XIV.

" Ay, the children of the chosen race
Shall carry and bring them to their place :
In the land of the Lord shall lead the same,
Bondsmen and handmaids.   Who shall blame,
When the slaves enslave, the oppressed ones o'er
The oppressor triumph for evermore ?

XV.

" God spoke, and gave us the word to keep :
Bade never fold the hands nor sleep
'Mid a faithless world,— at watch and ward,
Till the Christ at the end relieve our guard.
By his servant Moses the watch was set :
Though near upon cock-crow — we keep it yet.

XVI.

"Thou ! if thou wast He, who at mid-watch came,

By the starlight naming a dubious Name !

And if we were too heavy with sleep — too rash

With fear — O Thou, if that martyr-gash

Fell on thee coming to take thine own,

And we gave the Cross, when we owed the
    Throne —

XVII.

" Thou art the Judge.   We are bruised thus.

But, the judgment over, join sides with us !

Thine too is the cause ! and not more thine

Than ours, is the work of these dogs and swine,

Whose life laughs through and spits at their creed,

Who maintain thee in word, and defy thee in deed!

XVIII.

" We withstood Christ then ? be mindful how

At least we withstand Barabbas now !

Was our outrage sore ? but the worst we spared,

To have called these — Christians,— had we
    dared !

Let defiance of them, pay mistrust of thee,
And Rome make amends for Calvary !

XIX.

" By the torture, prolonged from age to age,
By the infamy, Israel's heritage,
By the Ghetto's plague, by the garb's disgrace,
By the badge of shame, by the felon's place,
By the branding-tool, the bloody whip,
And the summons to Christian fellowship,

XX.

" We boast our proofs, that at least the Jew
Would wrest Christ's name from the Devil's crew.
Thy face took never so deep a shade
But we fought them in it, God our aid
A trophy to bear, as we march, a band
South, east, and on the Pleasant Land ! "

[*The present Pope abolished this bad business of the
sermon.*—R. B.]

SOLILOQUY OF THE SPANISH CLOISTER.

I.

Gr-r-r — there go, my heart's abhorrence !
    Water your damned flower-pots, do !
If hate killed men, Brother Lawrence,
    God's blood, would not mine kill you !
What ? your myrtle-bush wants trimming ?
    Oh, that rose has prior claims —
Needs its leaden vase filled brimming ?
    Hell dry you up with its flames !

II.

At the meal we sit together :
    Salve tibi ! I must hear
Wise talk of the kind of weather,
    Sort of season, time of year :
Not a plenteous cork-crop : scarcely
    Dare we hope oak-galls, I doubt :
What's the Latin name for "parsley" ?
    What's the Greek name for Swine's Snout ?

III.

Whew !   We'll have our platter burnished,
 Laid with care on our own shelf !
With a fire-new spoon we're furnished,
 And a goblet for ourself,
Rinsed like something sacrificial
 Ere 'tis fit to touch our chaps —
Marked with L. for our initial !
 (He, he !   There his lily snaps !)

IV.

Saint, forsooth !   While brown Dolores
 Squats outside the Convent bank,
With Sanchicha, telling stories,
 Steeping tresses in the tank,
Blue-black, lustrous, thick like horsehairs,
 —Can't I see his dead eye glow
Bright, as 'twere a Barbary corsair's ?
 (That is, if he'd let it show !)

V.

When he finishes reflection,
 Knife and fork he never lays

Cross-wise, to my recollection,
　As do I, in Jesu's praise.
I, the Trinity illustrate,
　Drinking watered orange-pulp —
In three sips the Arian frustrate;
　While he drains his at one gulp!

VI.

Oh, those melons! If he's able
　We're to have a feast; so nice!
One goes to the Abbot's table,
　All of us get each a slice.
How go on your flowers? None double?
　Not one fruit-sort can you spy?
Strange! — And I, too, at such trouble,
　Keep 'em close-nipped on the sly!

VII.

There's a great text in Galatians,
　Once you trip on it, entails
Twenty-nine distinct damnations,
　One sure, if another fails.
If I trip him just a-dying,

Sure of Heaven as sure can be,
Spin him round and send him flying
Off to Hell, a Manichee?

VIII.

Or, my scrofulous French novel,
　On gray paper with blunt type!
Simply glance at it, you grovel
　Hand and foot in Belial's gripe:
If I double down its pages
　At the woeful sixteenth print,
When he gathers his greengages,
　Ope a sieve and slip it in't?

IX.

Or, there's Satan!—one might venture
　Pledge one's soul to him, yet leave
Such a flaw in the indenture
　As he'd miss till, past retrieve,
Blasted lay that rose-acacia
　We're so proud of! *Hy, Zy, Hine. . .*
'St, there's Vespers! *Plena gratiâ*
　Ave Virgo! Gr-r-r — you swine!

THE LABORATORY.

[*Ancien Régime.*]

I.

Now that I, tying thy glass mask tightly,

May gaze thro' these faint smokes curling whitely,

As thou pliest thy trade in this devil's-smithy —

Which is the poison to poison her, prithee ?

II.

He is with her ; and they know that I know

Where they are, what they do : they believe my

> tears flow

While they laugh, laugh at me, at me fled to the

> drear

Empty church, to pray God in, for them ! — I am

> here.

III.

Grind away, moisten and mash up thy paste,

Pound at thy powder, — I am not in haste !

Better sit thus, and observe thy strange things,
Than go where men wait me and dance at the
    King's.

IV.

That in the mortar — you call it a gum?
Ah, the brave tree whence such gold oozings come!
And yonder soft phial, the exquisite blue,
Sure to taste sweetly,— is that poison too?

V.

Had I but all of them, thee and thy treasures,
What a wild crowd of invisible pleasures!
To carry pure death in an earring, a casket,
A signet, a fan-mount, a filagree-basket!

VI.

Soon, at the King's, a mere lozenge to give
And Pauline should have just thirty minutes to
    live!
But to light a pastille, and Elise, with her head,
And her breast, and her arms, and her hands,
    should drop dead!

VII.

Quick — is it finished ? The color's too grim !
Why not soft like the phial's, enticing and dim ?
Let it brighten her drink, let her turn it and stir,
And try it and taste, ere she fix and prefer !

VIII.

What a drop ! She's not little, no minion like me —
That's why she ensnared him : this never will free
The soul from those strong, great eyes,— say, "no !"
To that pulse's magnificent come-and-go.

IX.

For only last night, as they whispered, I brought
My own eyes to bear on her so, that I thought
Could I keep them one half minute fixed, she would
    fall,
Shrivelled ; she fell not ; yet this does it all !

X.

Not that I bid you spare her the pain !
Let death be felt and the proof remain ;

Brand, burn up, bite into its grace —
He is sure to remember her dying face!

XI.

Is it done?   Take my mask off!   Nay, be not
    morose,
It kills her, and this prevents seeing it close :
The delicate droplet, my whole fortune's fee —
If it hurts her, beside, can it ever hurt me?

XII.

Now, take all my jewels, gorge gold to your fill,
You may kiss me, old man, on my mouth if you
    will!
But brush this dust off me, lest horror it brings
Ere I know it — next moment I dance at the King s!

A FORGIVENESS.

I am indeed the personage you know.
As for my wife,— what happened long ago —
You have a right to question me, as I
Am bound to answer.

            "Son, a fit reply!"
The monk half spoke, half ground through his
    clenched teeth,
At the confession-grate I knelt beneath.

Thus then all happened, Father! Power and place
I had as still I have. I ran life's race,
With the whole world to see, as only strains
His strength some athlete whose prodigious gains
Of good appall him : happy to excess,—
Work freely done should balance happiness
Fully enjoyed ; and, since beneath my roof
Housed she who made home heaven, in heaven's
    behoof

I went forth every day, and all day long
Worked for the world. Look, how the laborer's song
Cheers him ! Thus sang my soul, at each sharp
    throe
Of laboring flesh and blood — " She loves me so ! "

One day, perhaps such song so knit the nerve
That work grew play and vanished.   " I deserve
Haply my heaven an hour before the time ! "
I laughed, as silverly the clockhouse-chime
Surprised me passing through the postern-gate
— Not the main entry where the menials wait
And wonder why the world's affairs allow
The master sudden leisure.   That was how
I took the private garden-way for once.

Forth from the alcove, I saw start, ensconce
Himself behind the porphyry vase, a man.
My fancies in the natural order ran:
" A spy,— perhaps a foe in ambuscade,—
A thief,— more like, a sweetheart of some maid
Who pitched on the alcove for tryst perhaps."

"Stand there!" I bid.

          Whereat my man but wraps
His face the closelier with uplifted arm
Whereon the cloak lies, strikes in blind alarm
This and that pedestal as,—stretch and stoop,—
Now in, now out of sight, he thrids the group
Of statues, marble god and goddess ranged
Each side the pathway, till the gate's exchanged
For safety : one step thence, the street, you know !

Thus far I followed my gaze. Then, slow,
Near on admiringly, I breathed again,
And — back to that last fancy of the train —
" A danger risked for hope of just a word
With — which of all my nest may be the bird
This poacher covets for her plumage, pray ?
Carmen ? Juana ? Carmen seems too gay
For such adventure, while Juana's grave
— Would scorn the folly. I applaud the knave !
He had the eye, could single from my brood
His proper fledgling !"

As I turned, there stood
In face of me, my wife stone-still stone-white.
Whether one bound had brought her,— at first sight
Of what she judged the encounter, sure to be
Next moment, of the venturous man and me,—
Brought her to clutch and keep me from my prey,
Whether impelled because her death no day
Could come so absolutely opportune
As now at joy's height, like a year in June
Stayed at the fall of its first ripened rose ;
Or whether hungry for my hate — who knows ?—
Eager to end an irksome lie, and taste
Our tingling true relation, hate embraced
By hate one naked moment : — anyhow
There stone-still stone-white stood my wife, but now
The woman who made heaven within my house.
Ay, she who faced me was my very spouse
As well as love — you are to recollect !

"Stay !" she 'said. "Keep at least one soul un-
        specked
With crime, that's spotless hitherto — your own !

Kill me who court the blessing, who alone
Was, am and shall be guilty, first to last !
The man lay helpless in the toils I cast
About him, helpless as the statue there
Against that strangling bell-flower's bondage : tear
Away and tread to dust the parasite,
But do the passive marble no despite !
I love him as I hate you.   Kill me !   Strike
At one blow both infinitudes alike
Out of existence — hate and love !   Whence love ?
That's safe within my heart, nor will remove
For any searching of your steel, I think.
Whence hate ?   The secret lay on lip, at brink
Of speech, in one fierce tremble to escape,
At every form wherein your love took shape,
At each new provocation of your kiss.
Kill me ! "

      We went in.

                 Next day after this,
I felt as if the speech might come.   I spoke —
Easily, after all.

" The lifted cloak
Was screen sufficient: I concern myself
Hardly with laying hands on who for pelf —
Whate'er the ignoble kind — may prowl and brave
Cuffing and kicking proper to a knave
Detected by my household's vigilance.
Enough of such ! As for my love-romance —
I, like our good Hidalgo, rub my eyes
And wake and wonder how the film could rise
Which changed for me a barber's basin straight
Into — Mambrino's helm ? I hesitate
Nowise to say — God's sacramental cup !
Why should I blame the brass which, burnished up,
Will blaze, to all but me, as good as gold?
To me — a warning I was overbold
In judging metals. The Hidalgo waked
Only to die, if I remember, — staked
His life upon the basin's worth, and lost :
While I confess torpidity at most
In here and there a limb ; but, lame and halt,
Still should I work on, still repair my fault
Ere I took rest in death, — no fear at all !

Now, work — no word before the curtain fall ! "
The " curtain ? "   That of death on life, I meant :
My " word " permissible in death's event,
Would be — truth, soul to soul ; for, otherwise,
Day by day, three years long, there had to rise
And, night by night, to fall upon our stage —
Ours, doomed to public play by heritage —
Another curtain, when the world, perforce
Our critical assembly, in due course
Came and went, witnessing, gave praise or blame
To art-mimetic.   It had spoiled the game
If, suffered to set foot behind our scene,
The world had witnessed how stage-king and
        queen,
Gallant and lady, but a minute since
Enarming each the other, would evince
No sign of recognition as they took
His way and her way to whatever nook
Waited them in the darkness either side
Of that bright stage where lately groom and bride
Had fired the audience to a frenzy-fit
Of sympathetic rapture — every whit

Earned as the curtain fell on her and me,
— Actors.   Three whole years, nothing was to see
But calm and concord : where a speech was due
There came the speech ; when smiles were wanted too
Smiles were as ready.   In a place like mine,
Where foreign and domestic cares combine,
There's audience every day and all day long ;
But finally the last of the whole throng
Who linger lets one see his back.   For her —
Why, liberty and liking : I aver,
Liking and liberty !   For me — I breathed,
Let my face rest from every wrinkle wreathed
Smile-like about the mouth, unlearned my task
Of personation till next day bade mask,
And quietly betook me from that world
To the real world, not pageant : there unfurled
In work, its wings, my soul, the fretted power.
Three years I worked, each minute of each hour
Not claimed by acting : — work I may dispense
With talk about, since work in evidence,
Perhaps in history ; who knows or cares ?

After three years, this way, all unawares,

Our acting ended. She and I, at close

Of a loud night-feast, led, between two rows

Of bending male and female loyalty,

Our lord the king down staircase, while, held
    high

At arm's length did the twisted tapers' flare

Herald his passage from our palace where

Such visiting left glory evermore.

Again the ascent in public, till at door

As we two stood by the saloon — now blank

And disencumbered of its guests — there sank

A whisper in my ear, so low and yet

So unmistakable !

          "I half forget

The chamber you repair to, and I want

Occasion for one short word — if you grant

That grace — within a certain room you called

Our '*Study*,' for you wrote there while I scrawled

Some paper full of faces for my sport.

That room I can remember. Just one short

Word with you there, for the remembrance' sake !"

12

Follow me thither !" I replied.

                         We break
The gloom a little, as with guiding lamp
I lead the way, leave warmth and cheer, by damp
Blind disused serpentining ways afar
From where the habitable chambers are, —
Ascend, descend stairs tunnelled through the
      stone, —
Always in silence, — till I reach the lone
Chamber sepulchred for my very own
Out of the palace-quarry. When a boy,
Here was my fortress, stronghold from annoy,
Proof-positive of ownership; in youth
I garnered up my gleanings here — uncouth
But precious relics of vain hopes, vain fears ;
Finally, this became in after years
My closet of intrenchment to withstand
Invasion of the foe on every hand —
The multifarious herd in bower and hall,
State-room, — rooms whatsoe'er the style, which
      call

On masters to be mindful that, before

Men, they must look like men and something more.

Here,—when our lord the king's bestowment ceased

To deck me on the day that, golden-fleeced,

I touched ambition's height,—'twas here, released

From glory (always symbolled by a chain !)

No sooner was I privileged to gain

My secret domicile than glad I flung

That last toy on the table — gazed where hung

On hook my father's gift, the arquebuss —

And asked myself " Shall I envisage thus

The new prize and the old prize, when I reach

Another year's experience ? — own that each

Equalled   advantage — sportsman's — statesman s tool ?

That brought me down an eagle, this — a fool ! "

Into which room on entry, I set down

The lamp, and turning saw whose rustled gown

Had told me my wife followed, pace for pace.

Each of us looked the other in the face,

She spoke.   " Since I could die now . . ."

(To explain
Why that first struck me, know — not once again
Since the adventure at the porphyry's edge
Three years before, which sundered like a wedge
Her soul from mine,— though daily, smile to smile,
We stood before the public,— all the while
Not once had I distinguished, in that face
I paid observance to, the faintest trace
Of feature more than requisite for eyes
To do their duty by and recognize :
So did I force mine to obey my will
And pry no further.   There exists such skill,—
Those know who need it.   What physician shrinks
From needful contact with a corpse ?   He drinks
No plague so long as thirst for knowledge,— not
An idler impulse,— prompts inquiry.   What,
And will you disbelieve in power to bid
Our spirit back to bounds, as though we chid
A child from scrutiny that's just and right
In manhood ? Sense, not soul, accomplished sight,
Reported daily she it was — not how
Nor why a change had come to cheek and brow.)

"Since I could die now of the truth concealed,
Yet dare not, must not die,— so seems revealed
The Virgin's mind to me,— for death means
    peace,
Wherein no lawful part have I, whose lease
Of life and punishment the truth avowed
May haply lengthen,— let me push the shroud
Away, that steals to muffle ere is just
My penance-fire in snow ! I dare — I must
Live, by avowal of the truth — this truth —
I loved you ! Thanks for the fresh serpent's tooth
That, by a prompt new pang more exquisite
Than all preceding torture, proves me right !
I loved you yet I lost you ! May I go,
Burn to the ashes, now my shame you know ?"

I think there never was such — how express ? —
Horror coquetting with voluptuousness,
As in those arms of Eastern workmanship —
Yataghan, kandjar, things that rend and rip,
Gash rough, slash smooth, help hate so many ways,
Yet ever keep a beauty that betrays

Love still at work with the artificer
Throughout his quaint devising.   Why prefer,
Except for love's sake, that a blade should writhe
And bicker like a flame? — now play the scythe
As if some broad neck tempted,— now contract
And needle off into a fineness lacked
For just that puncture which the heart demands?
Then, such adornment! Wherefore need our hands
Enclose not ivory alone, nor gold
Roughened for use, but jewels? Nay, behold!
Fancy my favorite — which I seem to grasp
While I describe the luxury.   No asp
Is diapered more delicate round throat
Than this below the handle! These denote
— These mazy lines meandering, to end
Only in flesh they open — what intend
They else but water-purlings — pale contrast
With the life-crimson where they blend at last?
And mark the handle's dim pellucid green,
Carved, the hard jadestone, as you pinch a bean,
Into a sort of parrot-bird! He pecks
A grape-bunch ; his two eyes are ruby-specks

Pure from the mine ; seen this way,— glassy blank,

But turn them,— lo the inmost fire, that shrank

From sparkling, sends a red dart right to aim !

Why did I choose such toys ?   Perhaps the game

Of peaceful men is warlike, just as men

War-wearied get amusement from that pen

And paper we grow sick of — statesfolk tired

Of merely (when such measures are required)

Dealing out doom to people by three words,

A signature and seal : we play with swords

Suggestive of quick process.   That is how

I came to like the toys described you now,

Store of which glittered on the walls and strewed

The table, even, while my wife pursued

Her purpose to its ending.   " Now you know

This shame, my three years' torture, let me go,

Burn to the very ashes ! You — I lost,

Yet you — I loved ! "

                    The thing I pity most

In men is — action prompted by surprise

Of anger : men ? nay, bulls — whose onset lies

At instance of the firework and the goad !
Once the foe prostrate,— trampling once be-
     stowed,—
Prompt follows placability, regret,
Atonement.   Trust me, blood-warmth never yet
Betokened strong will ! As no leap of pulse
Pricked me, that first time, so did none convulse
My veins at this occasion for resolve.
Had that devolved which did not then devolve
Upon me, I had done — what now to do
Was quietly apparent.

         " Tell me who
The man was, crouching by the porphyry vase ! "
" No, never ! All was folly in his case,
All guilt in mine.   I tempted, he complied."

" And yet you loved me ?"

         " Loved you.   Double-dyed
In folly and in guilt, I thought you gave
Your heart and soul away from me to slave

At statecraft. Since my right in you seemed
 lost,
I stung myself to teach you, to your cost,
What you rejected could be prized beyond
Life, heaven, by the first fool I threw a fond
Look on, a fatal word to."

     " And you still
Love me ? Do I conjecture well or ill ? "

" Conjecture — well or ill ! I had three years
To spend in learning you."

     " We both are peers
In knowledge, therefore: since three years are spent
Ere thus much of yourself *I* learn — who went
Back to the house, that day, and brought my mind
To bear upon your action, uncombined
Motive from motive, till the dross, deprived
Of every purer particle, survived
At last in native simple hideousness,
Utter contemptibility, nor less

Nor more.   Contemptibility — exempt
How could I, from its proper due — contempt?
I have too much despised you to divert
My life from its set course by help or hurt
Of your all-despicable life — perturb
The calm I work in, by — men's mouth to curb,
Which at such news were clamorous enough —
Men's eyes to shut before my broidered stuff
With the huge hole there, my emblazoned wall
Blank where a scutcheon hung,— by, worse than all,
Each day's procession, my paraded life
Robbed and impoverished through the wanting wife
— Now that my life (which means — my work)
        was grown
Riches indeed !   Once, just this worth alone
Seemed work to have, that profit gained thereby
Of good and praise would — how rewardingly ! —
Fall at your feet,— a crown I hoped to cast
Before your love, my love should crown at last.
No love remaining to cast crown before,
My love stopped work now: but contempt the more
Impelled me task as ever head and hand,

Because the very fiends weave ropes of sand
Rather than taste pure hell in idleness.
Therefore I kept my memory down by stress
Of daily work I had no mind to stay
For the world's wonder at the wife away.
Oh, it was easy all of it, believe,

For I despised you ! But your words retrieve
Importantly the past. No hate assumed
The mask of love at any time ! There gloomed
A moment when love took hate's semblance, urged
By causes you declare ; but love's self purged
Away a fancied wrong I did both loves
— Yours and my own: by no hate's help, it proves,
Purgation was attempted. Then, you rise
High by how many a grade ! I did despise —
I do but hate you. Let hate's punishment
Replace contempt's ! First step to which ascent —
Write down your own words I re-utter you !
'*I loved my husband and I hated — who*
He was, I took up as my first chance, mere
Mud ball to fling and make love foul with !' Here
Lies paper ! "

"Would my blood for ink suffice!"

"It may · this minion from a land of spice,

Silk, feather — every bird of jewelled breast —

This poniard's beauty, ne'er so lightly prest

Above your heart there . ."

                "Thus?"

                        "It flows, I see.

Dip there the point and write!"

                      "Dictate to me!

Nay, I remember."

                And she wrote the words.

I read them.   Then —"Since love, in you, affords

License for hate, in me, to quench (I say)

Contempt — why, hate itself has passed away

In vengeance — foreign to contempt.   Depart

Peacefully to that death which Eastern art

Imbued this weapon with, if tales be true!

Love will succeed to hate.   I pardon you —

Dead in our chamber!"

                  True as truth the tale.

She died ere morning; then, I saw how pale

Her cheek was ere it wore day's paint-disguise,
And what a hollow darkened 'neath her eyes,
Now that I used my own.   She sleeps, as erst
Beloved, in this your church : ay, yours !

                              Immersed

In thought so deeply, Father ?   Sad, perhaps ?
For whose sake, hers or mine or his who wraps
— Still plain I seem to see !— about his head
The idle cloak,— about his heart (instead
Of cuirass) some fond hope he may elude
My vengeance in the cloister's solitude ?
Hardly, I think !   As little helped his brow
The cloak then, Father — as your grate helps now !

MEETING AT NIGHT.

I.

The gray sea and the long black land ;
And the yellow half-moon large and low ;
And the startled little waves that leap
In fiery ringlets from their sleep,
As I gain the cove with pushing prow,
And quench its speed in the slushy sand.

II.

Then a mile of warm sea-scented beach ;
Three fields to cross till a farm appears ;
A tap at the pane, the quick sharp scratch
And blue spurt of a lighted match,
And a voice less loud, thro' its joy and fears,
Than the two hearts beating each to each !

190

PARTING AT MORNING.

Round the cape of a sudden came the sea,
And the sun looked over the mountain's rim —
And straight was a path of gold for him,
And the need of a world of men for me.

THE ITALIAN IN ENGLAND.

That second time they hunted me
From hill to plain, from shore to sea,
And Austria, hounding far and wide
Her blood-hounds thro' the country side,
Breathed hot and instant on my trace,—
I made six days a hiding-place
Of that dry green old aqueduct
Where I and Charles, when boys, have plucked
The fire-flies from the roof above,
Bright creeping thro' the moss they love.
— How long it seems since Charles was lost !
Six days the soldiers crossed and crossed
The country in my very sight ;
And when that peril ceased at night
The sky broke out in red dismay
With signal-fires ; well, there I lay
Close covered o'er in my recess,
Up to the neck in ferns and cress,

Thinking on Metternich our friend,
And Charles's miserable end,
And much beside, two days ; the third,
Hunger o'ercame me when I heard
The peasants from the village go
To work among the maize ; you know,
With us, in Lombardy, they bring
Provisions packed on mules, a string
With little bells that cheer their task,
And casks, and boughs on every cask
To keep the sun's heat from the wine ;
These I let pass in jingling line,
And, close on them, dear noisy crew,
The peasants from the village, too ;
For at the very rear would troop
Their wives and sisters in a group
To help, I knew ; when these had passed,
I threw my glove to strike the last,
Taking the chance : she did not start,
Much less cry out, but stooped apart
One instant, rapidly glanced round,
And saw me beckon from the ground :

A wild bush grows and hides my crypt ;
She picked my glove up while she stripped
A branch off, then rejoined the rest
With that ; my glove lay in her breast :
Then I drew breath : they disappeared :
It was for Italy I feared.

An hour, and she returned alone
Exactly where my glove was thrown.
Meanwhile came many thoughts ; on me
Rested the hopes of Italy ;
I had devised a certain tale
Which, when 'twas told her, could not fail
Persuade the peasant of its truth ;
I meant to call a freak of youth
This hiding, and give hopes of pay,
And no temptations to betray.
But when I saw that woman's face,
Its calm simplicity of grace,
Our Italy's own attitude
In which she walked thus far, and stood,
Planting each naked foot so firm,

To crush the snake and spare the worm —

At first sight of her eyes, I said,

" I am that man upon whose head

They fix the price, because I hate

The Austrians over us : the State

Will give you gold — oh, gold so much,

If you betray me to their clutch !

And be your death, for aught I know,

If once they find you saved their foe.

Now, you must bring me food and drink,

And also paper, pen and ink,

And carry safe what I shall write

To Padua, which you'll reach at night

Before the Duomo shuts ; go in,

And wait till Tenebræ begin ;

Walk to the Third Confessional,

Between the pillar and the wall,

And kneeling whisper *whence comes peace ?*

Say it a second time ; then cease ;

And if the voice inside returns,

From Christ and Freedom ; what concerns

The cause of Peace ? — for answer, slip

My letter where you placed your lip ;
Then come back happy we have done
Our mother service — I, the son,
As you the daughter of our land ! "

   Three mornings more, she took her stand
In the same place, with the same eyes :
I was no surer of sun-rise
Than of her coming : we conferred
Of her own prospects, and I heard
She had a lover — stout and tall,
She said — then let her eyelids fall,
" He could do much "— as if some doubt
Entered her heart,— then, passing out ;
" She could not speak for others — who
Had other thoughts ; herself she knew : "
And so she brought me drink and food.
After four days, the scouts pursued
Another path : at last arrived
The help my Paduan friends contrived
To furnish me : she brought the news :
For the first time I could not choose

But kiss her hand and lay my own
Upon her head—" This faith was shown
" To Italy, our mother ; — she
Uses my hand and blesses thee ! "
She followed down to the sea-shore ;
I left and never saw her more.

　How very long since I have thought
Concerning — much less wished for — aught
Beside the good of Italy
For which I live and mean to die !
I never was in love ; and since
Charles proved false, nothing could convince
My inmost heart I had a friend ;
However, if I pleased to spend
Real wishes on myself — say, Three —
I know at least what one should be ;
I would grasp Metternich until
I felt his red wet throat distil
In blood thro' these two hands : and next,
— Nor much for that am I perplexed —
Charles, perjured traitor, for his part,

Should die slow of a broken heart
Under his new employers : last
— Ah, there, what should I wish ? For fast
Do I grow old and out of strength —
If I resolved to seek at length
My father's house again, how scared
They all would look, and unprepared !
My brothers live in Austria's pay
— Disowned me long ago, men say ;
And all my early mates who used
To praise me so — perhaps induced
More than one early step of mine —
Are turning wise ; while some opine
" Freedom grows License," some suspect
" Haste breeds Delay," and recollect
They always said, such premature
Beginnings never could endure !
So with a sullen " All's for best,"
The land seems settling to its rest.
I think, then, I should wish to stand
This evening in that dear, lost land,
Over the sea the thousand miles,

And know if yet that woman smiles
With the calm smile ; some little farm
She lives in there, no doubt ; what harm
If I sate on the door-side bench,
And while her spindle made a trench
Fantastically in the dust,
Inquired of all her fortunes — just
Her children's ages and their names,
And what may be the husband's aims
For each of them — I'd talk this out,
And sit there, for an hour about,
Then kiss her hand once more, and lay
Mine on her head, and go my way.

So much for idle wishing — how
It steals the time ! To business now !

UP AT A VILLA — DOWN IN THE CITY.

(As distinguished by an Italian person of quality.)

I.

Had I but plenty of money, money enough and
    to spare,
The house for me, no doubt, were a house in the
    city-square.
Ah, such a life, such a life, as one leads at the win-
    dow there !

II.

Something to see, by Bacchus, something to hear, at
    least !
There, the whole day long, one's life is a perfect
    feast ;
While up at a villa one lives, I maintain it, no
    more than a beast.

III.

Well now, look at our villa ! stuck like the horn of
a bull

Just on a mountain's edge as bare as the creature's
skull,

Save a mere shag of a bush with hardly a leaf to
pull !

— I scratch my own, sometimes, to see if the hair's
turned wool.

IV.

But the city, oh the city — the square with the
houses ! Why ?

They are stone-faced, white as a curd, there's something to take the eye !

Houses in four straight lines, not a single front awry !

You watch who crosses and gossips, who saunters,
who hurries by :

Green blinds, as a matter of course, to draw when
the sun gets high ;

And the shops with fanciful signs which are painted
properly.

V.

What of a villa ?   Though winter be over in March
    by rights,
'Tis May perhaps ere the snow shall have withered
    well off the heights :
You've the brown ploughed land before, where the
    oxen steam and wheeze,
And the hills over-smoked behind by the faint gray
    olive trees.

VI.

Is it better in May, I ask you ?   You've summer all
    at once ;
In a day he leaps complete with a few strong April
    suns !
'Mid the sharp short emerald wheat, scarce risen
    three fingers well,
The wild tulip, at end of its tube, blows out its
    great red bell,
Like a thin clear bubble of blood, for the children
    to pick and sell.

VII.

Is it ever hot in the square? There's a fountain to
    spout and splash !
In the shade it sings and springs ; in the shine such
    foam-bows flash
On the horses with curling fish-tails, that prance and
    and paddle and pash
Round the lady atop in the conch — fifty gazers do
    not abash,
Though all that she wears is some weeds round her
    waist in a sort of sash !

VIII.

All the year round at the villa, nothing's to see
    though you linger,
Except yon cypress that points like Death's lean
    lifted forefinger.
Some think fireflies pretty, when they mix in the
    corn and mingle,
Or thrid the stinking hemp till the stalks of it seem
    a-tingle.

Late August or early September, the stunning cicala
is shrill,
And the bees keep up their tiresome whine round
the resinous firs on the hill.
Enough of the seasons, — I spare you the months of
the fever and chill.

IX.

Ere opening your eyes in the city, the blessed
church-bells begin :
No sooner the bells leave off, than the diligence
rattles in ;
You get the pick of the news, and it costs you never
a pin.
By and by there's the traveling doctor gives pills,'
lets blood, draws teeth ;
Or the Pulcinello-trumpet breaks up the market
beneath.
At the post-office such a scene-picture — the new
play piping hot !
And a notice how only this morning, three liberal
thieves were shot.

Above it, behold the archbishop's most fatherly of
    rebukes,
And beneath, with his crown and his lion, some
    little new law of the Duke's !
Or a sonnet with flowery marge, to the Reverend
    Don So-and-so
Who is Dante, Boccacio, Petrarca, St. Jerome, and
    Cicero,
" And moreover," (the sonnet goes rhyming,) " the
    skirts of St. Paul has reached,
Having preached us those six Lent-lectures more
    unctuous than ever he preached."
Noon strikes, — here sweeps the procession ! our
    lady borne smiling and smart
With a pink gauze gown all spangles, and seven
    swords stuck in her heart !
Bang, whang, whang, goes the drum, *tootle-te-tootle*
    the fife ;
No keeping one's haunches still : it's the greatest
    pleasure in life.

X.

But bless you, it's dear — it's dear ! fowls, wine, at
    double the rate.

They have clapped a new tax upon salt, and what
    oil pays passing the gate

It's a horror to think of.   And so, the villa for me,
    not the city !

Beggars can scarcely be choosers — but still — ah,
    the pity, the pity !

Look, two and two go the priests, then the monks
    with cowls and sandals,

And the penitents dressed in white skirts, a-holding
    the yellow candles.

One, he carries a flag up straight, and another a
    cross with handles,

And the Duke's guard brings up the rear, for the
    better prevention of scandals.

Bang, whang, whang, goes the drum, *tootle-te-tootle*
    the fife.

Oh, a day in the city-square, there is no such pleas-
    ure in life !

THE ENGLISHMAN IN ITALY.

[*Piano di Sorrento.*]

Fortù, Fortù, my beloved one,
   Sit here by my side,
On my knees put up both little feet !
   I was sure, if I tried,
I could make you laugh spite of Scirocco :
   Now, open your eyes —
Let me keep you amused till he vanish
   In black from the skies,
With telling my memories over
   As you tell your beads ;
All the memories plucked at Sorrento
   — The flowers, or the weeds.

Time for rain ! for your long hot dry Autumn
   Had net-worked with brown
The white skin of each grape on the bunches
   Marked like a quail's crown,

Those creatures you make such account of,
　　Whose heads,— specked with white
Over brown like a great spider's back,
　　As I told you last night,—
Your mother bites off for her supper ;
　　Red-ripe as could be.

Pomegranates were chapping and splitting
　　In halves on the tree :
And betwixt the loose walls of great flintstone,
　　Or in the thick dust
On the path, or straight out of the rock side,
　　Wherever could thrust
Some burnt sprig of bold hardy rock-flower
　　Its yellow face up,
For the prize were great butterflies fighting,
　　Some five for one cup.
So, I guessed, ere I got up this morning,
　　What change was in store,
By the quick rustle-down of the quail-nets
　　Which woke me before

I could open my shutter, made fast
  With a bough and a stone,
And look thro' the twisted dead vine-twigs,
  Sole lattice that's known !
Quick and sharp ran the rings down the net-poles,
  While, busy beneath,
Your priest and his brother tugged at them,
  The rain in their teeth :
And out upon all the flat house-roofs
  Where split figs lay drying,
The girls took the frails under cover :
  Nor use seemed in trying
To get out the boats and go fishing,
  For, under the cliff,
Fierce the black water frothed o'er the blind-rock.
  No seeing our skiff
Arrive about noon from Amalfi,
  —Our fisher arrive,
And pitch down his basket before us,
  All trembling alive
With pink and gray jellies, your sea-fruit.
  —You touch the strange lumps,

14

And mouths gape there, eyes open, all manner
   Of horns and of humps,
Which only the fisher looks grave at,
   While round him like imps
Cling screaming the children as naked
   And brown as his shrimps ;
Himself too as bare to the middle —
   — You see round his neck
The string and its brass coin suspended,
   That saves him from wreck.
But to-day not a boat reached Salerno,
   So back to a man
Came our friends, with whose help in the vineyards
   Grape-harvest began :
In the vat, half-way up in our house-side,
   Like blood the juice spins,
While your brother all bare-legged is dancing
   Till breathless he grins
Dead-beaten, in effort on effort
   To keep the grapes under,
Since still when he seems all but master,
   In pours the fresh plunder

From girls who keep coming and going
  With basket on shoulder,
And eyes shut against the rain's driving,
  Your girls that are older,—
For under the hedges of aloe,
  And where, on its bed
Of the orchard's black mould, the love-apple
  Lies pulpy and red,
All the young ones are kneeling and filling
  Their laps with the snails
Tempted out by this first rainy weather,—
  Your best of regales,
As to-night will be proved to my sorrow,
  When, supping in state,
We shall feast our grape-gleaners (two dozen,
  Three over one plate)
With lasagne so tempting to swallow
  In slippery ropes,
And gourds fried in great purple slices,
  That color of popes.
Meantime, see the grape-bunch they've brought
  you,—

The rain-water slips
O'er the heavy blue bloom on each globe
    Which the wasp to your lips
Still follows with fretful persistence —
    Nay, taste, while awake,
This half of a curd-white smooth cheese-ball,
    That peels, flake by flake,
Like an onion's, each smoother and whiter;
    Next, sip this weak wine
From the thin green glass flask, with its stopper,
    A leaf of the vine,—
And end with the prickly-pear's red flesh
    That leaves thro' its juice
The stony black seeds on your pearl-teeth
    . . Scirocco is loose!
Hark! the quick, whistling pelt of the olives
    Which thick in one's track,
Tempt the stranger to pick up and bite them,
    Tho' not yet half black!
How the old twisted olive trunks shudder!
    The medlars let fall
Their hard fruit, and the brittle great fig-trees

Snap off, figs and all,—
For here comes the whole of the tempest!
˙ No refuge, but creep
Back again to my side and my shoulder,
    And listen or sleep.

O how will your country show next week,
    When all the vine-boughs
Have been stripped of their foliage to pasture
    The mules and the cows?
Last eve, I rode over the mountains;
    Your brother, my guide,
Soon left me, to feast on the myrtles
    That offered, each side,
Their fruit-balls, black, glossy and luscious,—
    Or strip from the sorbs
A treasure, so rosy and wondrous
    Of hairy gold orbs!
But my mule picked his sure, sober path out,
    Just stopping to neigh
When he recognized down in the valley
    His mates on their way

With the faggots, and barrels of water ;
　And soon we emerged
From the plain, where the woods could scarce fol-
　　　low ;
　And still as we urged
Our way, the woods wondered, and left us,
　As up still we trudged
Though the wild path grew wilder each instant,
　And place was e'en grudged
'Mid the rock-chasms, and piles of loose stones
　(Like the loose broken teeth
Of some monster, which climbed there to die
　From the ocean beneath)
Place was grudged to the silver-gray fume-weed
　That clung to the path,
And dark rosemary, ever a-dying,
　That, 'spite the wind's wrath,
So loves the salt rock's face to seaward,—
　And lentisks as staunch
To the stone where they root and bear berries,—
　And . . . what shows a branch
Coral-colored, transparent, with circlets

Of pale sea-green leaves —
Over all trod my mule with the caution
    Of gleaners o'er sheaves,
Still, foot after foot like a lady —
    So, round after round,
He climbed to the top of Calvano,
    And God's own profound
Was above me, and round me the mountains,
    And under, the sea,
And within me, my heart to bear witness
    What was and shall be !
Oh heaven, and the terrible crystal !
    No rampart excludes
Your eye from the life to be lived
    In the blue solitudes !
Oh, those mountains, their infinite movement !
    Still moving with you —
For, ever some new head and breast of them
    Thrusts into view
To observe the intruder — you see it
    If quickly you turn
And, before they escape you, surprise them —

They grudge you should learn

How the soft plains they look on, lean over,

    And love (they pretend)

—Cower beneath them ; the flat sea-pine crouches,

    The wild fruit-trees bend,

E'en the myrtle-leaves curl, shrink and shut —

    All is silent and grave —

'Tis a sensual and timorous beauty —

    How fair, but a slave !

So, I turned to the sea,— and there slumbered

    As greenly as ever

Those isles of the siren, your Galli ;

    No ages can sever

The Three, nor enable their sister

    To join them,— half way

On the voyage, she looked at Ulysses —

    No farther to-day ;

Tho' the small one, just launched in the wave,

    Watches breast-high and steady

From under the rock, her bold sister

    Swum half-way already.

Fortù, shall we sail there together

And see from the sides

Quite new rocks show their faces — new haunts

    Where the siren abides?

Shall we sail round and round them, close over

    The rocks, tho' unseen,

That ruffle the gray glassy water

    To glorious green?

Then scramble from splinter to splinter

    Reach land and explore,

On the largest, the strange square black turret

    With never a door,

Just a loop to admit the quick lizards;

    Then, stand there and hear

The birds' quiet singing, that tells us

    What life is, so clear!

The secret they sang to Ulysses,

    When, ages ago,

He heard and he knew this life's secret,

    I hear and I know!

Ah, see! The sun breaks o'er Calvano —

    He strikes the great gloom

And flutters it o'er the mount's summit
   In airy gold fume!
All is over!   Look out, see the gypsy,
   Our tinker and smith,
Has arrived, set up bellows and forge,
   And down-squatted forthwith
To his hammering, under the wall there;
   One eye keeps aloof
The urchins that itch to be putting
   His jews'-harps to proof,
While the other, thro' locks of curled wire,
   Is watching how sleek
Shines the hog, come to share in the windfalls
   —An abbot's own cheek!
All is over!   Wake up and come out now,
   And down let us go,
And see the fine things got in order
   At Church for the show
Of the Sacrament, set forth this evening;
   To-morrow's the Feast
Of the Rosary's Virgin, by no means
   Of Virgins the least —

As you'll hear in the off-hand discourse
  Which (all nature, no art)
The Dominican brother, these three weeks,
  Was getting by heart.
Not a post nor a pillar but's dizened
  With red and blue papers ;
All the roof waves with ribbons, each altar
  A-blaze with long tapers ;
But the great masterpiece is the scaffold
  Rigged glorious to hold
All the fiddlers and fifers and drummers,
  And trumpeters bold,
Not afraid of Bellini nor Auber,
  Who, when the priest's hoarse,
Will strike us up something that's brisk
  For the feast's second course.
And then will the flaxen-wigged Image
  Be carried in pomp
Thro' the plain, while in gallant procession
  The priests mean to stomp.
And all round the glad church lie old bottles
  With gunpowder stopped,

Which will be, when the Image re-enters,
  Religiously popped.
And at night from the crest of Calvano
  Great bonfires will hang,
On the plain will the trumpets join chorus,
  And more poppers bang!
At all events, come — to the garden,
  As far as the wall
See me tap with a hoe on the plaster
  Till out there shall fall
A scorpion with wide angry nippers!

  . . . " Such trifles "—you say?
Fortù, in my England at home,
  Men meet gravely to-day
And debate, if abolishing Corn-laws
  Is righteous and wise
— If 'tis proper, Scirocco should vanish
  In black from the skies!

HOME-THOUGHTS FROM ABROAD.

I.

Oh, to be in England
Now that April's there,
And whoever wakes in England
Sees, some morning, unaware,
That the lowest boughs and the brush-wood sheaf
Round the elm-tree bole are in tiny leaf,
While the chaffinch sings on the orchard bough
In England — now !

II.

And after April, when May follows,
And the whitethroat builds, and all the swallows —
Hark ! where my blossomed pear-tree in the hedge
Leans to the field and scatters on the clover
Blossoms and dewdrops — at the bent spray's edge—
That's the wise thrush ; he sings each song twice
    over,

Lest you should think he never could recapture
The first fine careless rapture !
And though the fields look rough with hoary dew,
All will be gay when noontide wakes anew
The buttercups, the little children's dower,
— Far brighter than this gaudy melon-flower !

THE GUARDIAN-ANGEL:

A Picture at Fano.

I.

Dear and great Angel, wouldst thou only leave
  That child, when thou hast done with him, for me!
Let me sit all the day here, that when eve
  Shall find performed thy special ministry
And time come for departure, thou, suspending
'Thy flight, mayst see another child for tending,
Another-still, to quiet and retrieve.

II.

Then I shall feel thee step one step, no more,
  From where thou standest now, to where I gaze,
And suddenly my head be covered o'er
  With those wings, white above the child who prays
Now on that tomb — and I shall feel thee guarding
  Me, out of all the world; for me, discarding
Yon heaven thy home, that waits and opes its door!

223

III.

I would not look up thither past thy head
   Because the door opes, like that child, I know,
For I should have thy gracious face instead,
   Thou bird of God ! And wilt thou bend me low
Like him, and lay, like his, my hands together,
And lift them up to pray, and gently tether
   Me, as thy lamb there, with thy garment's spread ?

IV.

If this was ever granted, I would rest
   My head beneath thine, while thy healing hands
Close-covered both my eyes beside thy breast,
   Pressing the brain, which too much thought ex-
      pands,
Back to its proper size again, and smoothing
Distortion down till every nerve had soothing,
   And all lay quiet, happy and supprest.

V.

How soon all worldly wrong would be repaired !
   I think how I should view the earth and skies

And sea, when once again my brow was bared
　After thy healing, with such different eyes.
O, world, as God has made it ! all is beauty :
And knowing this, is love, and love is duty.
　What further may be sought for or declared ?

VI.

Guercino drew this angel I saw teach
　(Alfred, dear friend) — that little child to pray,
Holding the little hands up, each to each
　Pressed gently, — with his own head turned away
Over the earth where so much lay before him
Of work to do, though heaven was opening o'er him,
　And he was left at Fano by the beach.

VII.

We were at Fano, and three times we went
　To sit and see him in his chapel there,
And drink his beauty to our soul's content
　— My angel with me too : and since I care
For dear Guercino's fame, (to which in power
And glory comes this picture for a dower,
　Fraught with a pathos so magnificent)

15

VIII.

And since he did not work so earnestly
   At all times, and has else endured some wrong,—
I took one thought his picture struck from me,
   And spread it out, translating it to song.
My Love is here.   Where are you, dear old friend?
How rolls the Wairoa at your world's far end?
   This is Ancona, yonder is the sea.

SONG.

I.

Nay but you, who do not love her,
   Is she not pure gold, my mistress?
Holds earth aught — speak truth — above her?
   Aught like this tress, see, and this tress,
And this last fairest tress of all,
So fair, see, ere I let it fall!

II.

Because, you spend your lives in praising;
   To praise, you search the wide world over;
So, why not witness, calmly gazing,
   If earth holds aught — speak truth — above her?
Above this tress, and this I touch
But cannot praise, I love so much!

227

EVELYN HOPE.

I.

Beautiful Evelyn Hope is dead !
   Sit and watch by her side an hour.
That is her book-shelf, this her bed ;
   She plucked that piece of geranium-flower,
Beginning to die too, in the glass.
   Little has yet been changed, I think —
The shutters are shut, no light may pass
   Save two long rays thro' the hinge's chink.

II.

Sixteen years old when she died !
   Perhaps she had scarcely heard my name —
It was not her time to love : beside,
   Her life had many a hope and aim,
Duties enough and little cares,
   And now was quiet, and now astir —
Till God's hand beckoned unawares,
   And the sweet little brow is all of her.

III.

Is it too late then, Evelyn Hope?

    What, your soul was pure and true,

The good stars met in your horoscope,

    Made you of spirit, fire and dew —

And just because I was thrice as old,

    And our paths in the world diverged so wide,

Each was nought to each, must I be told?

    We were fellow mortals, nought beside?

IV.

No, indeed! for God above

    Is great to grant, as mighty to make,

And creates the love to reward the love,—

    I claim you still, for my own love's sake!

Delayed it may be for more lives yet,

    Through worlds I shall traverse, not a few —

Much is to learn and much to forget

    Ere the time be come for taking you.

V.

But the time will come,— at last it will,

    When, Evelyn Hope, what meant, I shall say,

In the lower earth, in the years long still,
    That body and soul so pure and gay?
Why your hair was amber, I shall divine —
    And your mouth of your own geranium's red —
And what you would do with me, in fine,
    In the new life come in the old one's stead.

VI.

I have lived, I shall say, so much since then,
    Given up myself so many times,
Gained me the gains of various men,
    Ransacked the ages, spoiled the climes;
Yet one thing, one, in my soul's full scope,
    Either I missed or itself missed me —
And I want and find you, Evelyn Hope!
    What is the issue? let us see!

VII.

I loved you, Evelyn, all the while;
    My heart seemed full as it could hold —
There was space and to spare for the frank young
        smile
    And the red young mouth and the hairs' young
        gold.

So, hush, — I will give you this leaf to keep —
  See, I shut it inside the sweet cold band.
There, that is our secret ! go to sleep ;
  You will wake, and remember, and understand.

ABT VOGLER.

(After he has been extemporizing upon the instrument of his invention.)

I.

Would that the structure brave, the manifold music
  I build,
  Bidding my organ obey, calling its keys to their
    work,
Claiming each slave of the sound, at a touch, as
    when Solomon willed
  Armies of angels that soar, legions of demons that
    lurk,
Man, brute, reptile, fly,— alien of end and of aim,
  Adverse, each from the other heaven-high, hell-
    deep removed,—
Should rush into sight at once as he named the
    ineffable Name,
  And pile him a palace straight, to pleasure the
    princess he loved !

II.

Would it might tarry like his, the beautiful building
  of mine,
  This which my keys in a crowd pressed and impor-
  tuned to raise !
Ah, one and all, how they helped, would dispart
  now and now combine,
  Zealous to hasten the work, heighten their master
  his praise !
And one would bury his brow with a wild plunge
  down to hell,
  Burrow a while and build, broad on the roots of
  things,
Then up again swim into sight, having based me
  my palace well,
  Founded it, fearless of flame, flat on the nether
  springs.

III.

And another would mount and march, like the excellent minion he was,
  Ay, another and yet another, one crowd but with
  many a crest,

Raising my rampired walls of gold as transparent as
　　glass,
　　Eager to do and die, yield each his place to the
　　　rest :
For higher still and higher, as a runner tips with
　　fire
When a great illumination surprises a festal night —
Outlining round and round Rome's dome from space
　　to spire,
　　Up, the pinnacled glory reached, and the pride of
　　　my soul was in sight.

IV.

In sight ? Not half ! for it seemed, it was certain, to
　　match man's birth,
　　Nature in turn conceived, obeying an impulse as I ;
And the emulous heaven yearned down, made effort
　　to reach the earth,
　　As the earth had done her best, in my passion, to
　　　scale the sky :
Novel splendors burst forth, grew familiar, and
　　dwelt with mine,

Not a point nor peak but found and fixed its wan-
    dering star ;

Meteor-moons, balls of blaze : and they did not pale
    nor pine,

For earth had attained to heaven, there was no
    more near nor far.

v.

Nay, more ; for there wanted not who walked in the
    glare and glow,

    Presences plain in the place ; or, fresh from the
        Protoplast,

Furnished for ages to come, when a kindlier wind
    should blow,

    Lured now to begin and live, in a house to their
        liking at last ;

Or else the wonderful Dead who have passed
    through the body and gone,

    But were back once more to breathe in an old
        world worth their new :

What never had been, was now ; what was, as it
    shall be anon ;
And what is,— shall I say, matched both ? for I
    was made perfect too.

VI.

All through my keys that gave their sounds to a
    wish of my soul,
  All through my soul that praised as its wish
    flowed visibly forth,
All through music and me ! For think, had I
    painted the whole,
  Why, there it had stood, to see, nor the process
    so wonder-worth :
Had I written the same, made verse — still, effect
    proceeds from cause,
  Ye know why the forms are fair, ye hear how the
    tale is told ;
It is all triumphant art, but art in obedience to
    laws,
  Painter and poet are proud in the artist-list en-
    rolled: —

VII.

But here is the finger of God, a flash of the will
    that can,
  Existent behind all laws, that made them, and,
    lo, they are !
And I know not if, save in this, such gift be allowed
    to man,
  That out of three sounds he frame, not a fourth
    sound, but a star.
Consider it well : each tone of our scale in itself is
    naught ;
  It is everywhere in the world, — loud, soft, and
    all is said :
Give it to me to use ! I mix it with two in my
    thought;
  And, there ! Ye have heard and seen : consider
    and bow the head !

VIII.

Well, it is gone at last, the palace of music I reared ;
  Gone! and the good tears start, the praises that
    come too slow ;

For one is assured at first, one scarce can say that
    he feared,
  That he even gave it a thought, the gone thing
    was to go.
Never to be again !   But many more of the kind
  As good, nay, better perchance : is this your
    comfort to me ?
To me, who must be saved because I cling with my
    mind
  To the same, same self, same love, same God :
    ay, what was, shall be.

IX.

Therefore to whom turn I but to Thee, the ineffable
    Name ?
  Builder and Maker, Thou, of houses not made
    with hands !
What, have fear of change from Thee, who art ever
    the same ?
  Doubt that Thy power can fill the heart that Thy
    power expands ?

There shall never be one lost good ! What was,
    shall live as before ;
  The evil is null, is naught, is silence implying
    sound ;
What was good, shall be good, with, for evil, so
    much good more ;
  On the earth the broken arcs ; in the heaven a
    perfect round.

x.

All we have willed or hoped or dreamed of good,
    shall exist ;
  Not its likeness, but itself ; no beauty, nor good,
    nor power
Whose voice has gone forth, but each survives for
    the melodist
When eternity affirms the conception of an hour.
The high that proved too high, the heroic for earth
    too hard,
  The passion that left the ground to lose itself in
    the sky,

Are music sent up to God by the lover and the
    bard;
    Enough that He heard it once : we shall hear it
        by and by.

XI.

And what is our failure here but a triumph's evi-
    dence
    For the fulness of the days?   Have we withered
        or agonized?
Why else was the pause prolonged but that singing
    might issue thence?
    Why rushed the discords in, but that harmony
        should be prized?
Sorrow is hard to bear, and doubt is slow to
    clear,
    Each sufferer says his say, his scheme of the weal
        and woe :
But God has a few of us whom He whispers in the
    ear;
    The rest may reason and welcome, 'tis we musi-
        cians know.

XII.

Well, it is earth with me ; silence resumes her reign :

I will be patient and proud and soberly acqui-
esce —

Give me the keys — I feel for the common chord
again,

Sliding by semitones, till I sink to the minor,—
yes,

And I blunt it into a ninth, and I stand on alien
ground,

Surveying awhile the heights I rolled from into
the deep ;

Which, hark, I have dared and done, for my resting-
place is found,

The C Major of this life : so, now I will try to
sleep.

SAUL.

I.

Said Abner, " At last thou art come ! Ere I tell,
ere thou speak,

Kiss my cheek, wish me well ! " Then I wished it,
and did kiss his cheek.

And he, "Since the King, O my friend, for thy
countenance sent,

Neither drunken nor eaten have we ; nor until from
his tent

Thou return with the joyful assurance the King
liveth yet,

Shall our lip with the honey be bright, with the
water be wet.

For out of the black mid-tent's silence, a space of
three days,

Not a sound hath escaped to thy servants, of prayer
or of praise,

To betoken that Saul and the Spirit have ended
their strife,

And that, faint in his triumph, the monarch sinks
back upon life.

II.

" Yet now my heart leaps, O beloved ! God's child,
with his dew

On thy gracious gold hair, and those lilies still
living and blue

Just broken to twine round thy harp-strings, as if no
wild heat

Were now raging to torture the desert ! "

III.

Then I, as was meet,

Knelt down to the God of my fathers, and rose on
my feet,

And ran o'er the sand burnt to powder. The tent
was unlooped ;

I pulled up the spear that obstructed, and under I
    stooped ;

Hands and knees on the slippery grass-patch, all
    withered and gone,

That extends to the second inclosure, I groped my
    way on

Till I felt where the foldskirts fly open. Then once
    more I prayed,

And opened the foldskirts and entered, and was
    not afraid,

But spoke, "Here is David, thy servant !" And no
    voice replied.

At the first I saw nought but the blackness — but
    soon I descried

A something more black than the blackness — the
    vast, the upright

Main prop which sustains the pavilion : and slow
    into sight

Grew a figure against it, gigantic and blackest of
    all ; —

Then a sunbeam, that burst thro' the tent-roof, —
    showed Saul.

IV.

He stood as erect as that tent-prop ; both arms
  stretched out wide

On the great cross-support in the centre, that goes
  to each side :

He relaxed not a muscle, but hung there,—as,
  caught in his pangs

And waiting his change the king-serpent all heavily
  hangs,

Far away from his kind, in the pine, till deliverance
  come

With the spring-time,—so agonized Saul, drear and
  stark, blind and dumb.

V.

Then I tuned my harp,—took off the lilies we twine
  round its chords

Lest they snap 'neath the stress of the noontide —
  those sunbeams like swords !

And I first played the tune all our sheep know, as,
  one after one,

So docile they come to the pen-door, till folding be
  done.

They are white and untorn by the bushes, for lo,
　　they have fed
Where the long grasses stifle the water within the
　　stream's bed ;
And now one after one seeks its lodging, as star
　　follows star
Into eve and the blue far above us,— so blue and so
　　far !

VI.

—Then the tune, for which quails on the cornland
　　will each leave his mate
To fly after the player; then, what makes the
　　crickets elate,
Till for boldness they fight one another : and then,
　　what has weight　　　　　　　　　　[house—
To set the quick jerboa a-musing outside his sand
There are none such as he for a wonder, half bird and
　　half mouse ! —
God made all the creatures and gave them our love
　　and our fear,
To give sign, we and they are his children, one
　　family here.

VII.

Then I played the help-tune of our reapers, their
    wine-song, when hand

Grasps at hand, eye lights eye in good friendship,
    and great hearts expand

And grow one in the sense of this world's life. —
    And then, the last song

When the dead man is praised on his journey —
    " Bear, bear him along

With his few faults shut up like dead flowerets ! are
    balm-seeds not here

To console us? The land has none left, such as he
    on the bier.

Oh, would we might keep thee, my brother ! " —
    And then, the glad chaunt

Of the marriage, — first go the young maidens, next,
    she whom we vaunt

As the beauty, the pride of our dwelling. — And
    then, the great march

Wherein man runs to man to assist him and buttress
    an arch

Nought can break ; who shall harm them, our friends ?

— Then, the chorus intoned

As the Levites go up to the altar in glory en-
throned . . .

But I stopped here — for here in the darkness, Saul
groaned.

VIII.

And I paused, held my breath in such silence, and
listened apart ;

And the tent shook, for mighty Saul shuddered, —
and sparkles 'gan dart

From the jewels that woke in his turban at once
with a start —

All its lordly male-sapphires, and rubies courageous
at heart.

So the head — but the body still moved not, still
hung there erect.

And I bent once again to my playing, pursued it
unchecked,

As I sang, —

IX.

" Oh, our manhood's prime vigor ! no spirit feels
waste,

Not a muscle is stopped in its playing, nor sinew
  unbraced.

Oh, the wild joys of living! the leaping from rock
  up to rock —

The strong rending of boughs from the fir-tree,—
  the cool silver shock

Of the plunge in a pool's living water,— the hunt of
  the bear,

And the sultriness showing the lion is couched in
  his lair.

And the meal — the rich dates — yellowed over
  with gold dust divine,

And the locust's-flesh steeped in the pitcher ; the
  full draught of wine,

And the sleep in the dried river-channel where bull-
  rushes tell

That the water was wont to go warbling so softly
  and well.

How good is man's life, the mere living ! how fit to
  employ

All the heart and the soul and the senses, forever in
  joy ?

Hast thou loved the white locks of thy father, whose
    sword thou didst guard
When he trusted thee forth with the armies, for
    glorious reward ?
Didst thou see the thin hands of thy mother, held
    up as men sung
The low song of the nearly-departed, and heard her
    faint tongue
Joining in while it could to the witness, " Let one
    more attest,
I have lived, seen God's hand thro' a lifetime, and
    all was for best . . ."
Then they sung thro' their tears in strong triumph
    not much,— but the rest.
And thy brothers, the help and the contest, the
    working whence grew
Such result as from seething grape-bundles, the
    spirit strained true !
And the friends of thy boyhood — that boyhood of
    wonder and hope,
Present promise, and wealth of the future beyond
    the eye's scope,—

Till lo, thou art grown to a monarch ; a people is
    thine ;

And all gifts which the world offers singly, on one
    head combine !

On one head, all the beauty and strength, love and
    rage, like the throe

That, a-work in the rock, helps its labor, and lets
    the gold go :

High ambition and deeds which surpass it, fame
    crowning it,— all

Brought to blaze on the head of one creature —
    King Saul ! "

X.

And lo, with that leap of my spirit, heart, hand,
    harp and voice,

Each lifting Saul's name out of sorrow, each bidding
    rejoice

Saul's fame in the light it was made for — as when,
    dare I say,

The Lord's army in rapture of service, strains
    through its array,

And upsoareth the cherubim-chariot — " Saul !"
    cried I, and stopped,

And waited the thing that should follow. Then
    Saul, who hung propt

By the tent's cross-support in the centre, was struck
    by his name.

Have ye seen when Spring's arrowy summons goes
    right to the aim,

And some mountain, the last to withstand her, that
    held, (he alone,

While the vale laughed in freedom and flowers) on
    a broad bust of stone

A year's snow bound about for a breastplate,—
    leaves grasp of the sheet?

Fold on fold all at once it crowds thunderously
    down to his feet,

And there fronts you, stark, black but alive yet,
    your mountain of old,

With his rents, the successive bequeathings of ages
    untold —

Yea, each harm got in fighting your battles, each
    furrow and scar

Of his head thrust 'twixt you and the tempest —
 all hail, there they are !
Now again to be softened with verdure, again hold
 the nest
Of the dove, tempt the goat and its young to the
 green on its crest
For their food in the ardors of summer !   One long
 shudder thrilled
All the tent till the very air tingled, then sank and
 was stilled,
At the King's self left standing before me, released
 and aware.
What was gone, what remained ? all to traverse
 'twixt hope and despair —
Death was past, life not come — so he waited.
 Awhile his right hand
Held the brow, helped the eyes left too vacant forth-
 with to remand
To their place what new objects should enter :
 'twas Saul as before.
I looked up and dared gaze at those eyes, nor was
 hurt any more

Than by slow pallid sunsets in autumn, ye watch
  from the shore

At their sad level gaze o'er the ocean — a sun's slow
  decline

Over hills which, resolved in stern silence, o'erlap
  and entwine

Base with base to knit strength more intense : so,
  arm folded in arm

O'er the chest whose slow heavings subsided.

XI.

  What spell or what charm,

(For awhile there was trouble with me) what next
  should I urge

To sustain him where song had restored him? —
  Song filled to the verge

His cup with the wine of this life, pressing all that
  it yields

Of mere fruitage, the strength and the beauty ! Beyond, on what fields,

Glean a vintage more potent and perfect to brighten
  the eye

And bring blood to the lip, and commend them the
　　cup they put by ?

He saith, " It is good ; still he drinks not — he lets
　　me praise life,

Gives assent, yet would die for his own part.

XII.

　　　　　　　Then fancies grew rife

Which had come long ago on the pastures, when
　　round me the sheep,

Fed in silence — above, the one eagle wheeled slow
　　as in sleep,

And I lay in my hollow, and mused on the world
　　that might lie

'Neath his ken, though I saw but the strip 'twixt
　　the hill and the sky :

And I laughed — " Since my days are ordained to
　　be passed with my flocks,

Let me people at least with my fancies, the plains
　　and the rocks,

Dream the life I am never to mix with, and image
　　the show

Of mankind as they live in those fashions I hardly
. shall know !

Schemes of life, its best rules and right uses, the
courage that gains,

And the prudence that keeps what men strive for."
And now these old trains

Of vague thought came again ; I grew surer ; so
once more the string

Of my harp made response to my spirit, as thus —

XIII.

"Yea, my king,"

I began — "thou dost well in rejecting mere com-
forts that spring

From the mere mortal life held in common by man
and by brute :

In our flesh grows the branch of this life, in our
soul it bears fruit.

Thou hast marked the slow rise of the tree, — how
its stem trembled first

Till it passed the kid's lip, the stag's antler ; then
safely outburst

The fan-branches all round ; and thou mindedst
    when these too, in turn

Broke a-bloom and the palm-tree seemed perfect ;
    yet more was to learn,

Ev'n the good that comes in with the palm-fruit.
    Our dates shall we slight,

When their juice brings a cure for all sorrows ? or
    care for the plight

Of the palm's self whose slow growth produced
    them ? Not so ! stem and branch

Shall decay, nor be known in their place, while the
    palm-wine shall staunch

Every wound of man's spirit in winter. I pour thee
    such wine.

Leave the flesh to the fate it was fit for ! the spirit
    be thine !

By the spirit, when age shall p'ercome thee, thou
    still shalt enjoy

More indeed, than at first when inconscious, the
    life of a boy.

Crush that life, and behold its wine running ! each
    deed thou hast done

17

Dies, revives, goes to work in the world ; until e'en
  as the sun

Looking down on the earth, though clouds spoil
  him, though tempests efface,

Can find nothing his own deed produced not, must
  everywhere trace

The results of his past summer-prime,— so, each
  ray of thy will,

Every flash of thy passion and prowess, long over,
  shall thrill

Thy whole people the countless, with ardor, till
  they too give forth

A like cheer to their sons, who in turn, fill the south
  and the north

With the radiance thy deed was the germ of.   Carouse in the past.

But the license of age has its limit ; thou diest at
  last.

As the lion when age dims his eye-ball, the rose at
  her height,

So with man — so his power and his beauty forever
  take flight.

No ! again a long draught of my soul-wine ! look
    forth o'er the years —

Thou hast done now with eyes for the actual ; be-
    gin with the seer's !

Is Saul dead ? in the depth of the vale make his
    tomb — bid arise

A gray mountain of marble heaped four-square, till
    built to the skies.

Let it mark where the great First King slumbers —
    whose fame would ye know ?

Up above see the rock's naked face, where the
    record shall go

In great characters cut by the scribe,— Such was
    Saul, so he did ;

With the sages directing the work, by the populace
    chid,—

For not half, they'll affirm, is comprised there !
    Which fault to amend,

In the grove with his kind grows the cedar, whereon
    they shall spend

(See, in tablets 'tis level before them) their praise,
    and record

With the gold of the graver, Saul's story,— the
    statesman's great word

Side by side with the poet's sweet comment. The
    river's a-wave

With smooth paper-reeds grazing each other when
    prophet winds rave :

So the pen gives unborn generations their due and
    their part

In thy being ! Then, first of the mighty, thank God
    that thou art."

XIV.

And behold while I sang —- But O Thou who didst
    grant me that day,

And before it not seldom hast granted, thy help to
    essay

Carry on and complete an adventure,— my Shield
    and my Sword

In that act where my soul was thy servant, thy word
    was my word,—

Still be with me, who then at the summit of human
    endeavor

And scaling the highest man's thought could, gazed
    hopeless as ever

On the new stretch of Heaven above me — till,
    Mighty to save,

Just one lift of thy hand cleared that distance —
    God's throne from man's grave !

Let me tell out my tale to its ending — my voice to
    my heart,

Which can scarce dare believe in what marvels that
    night I took part,

As this morning I gather the fragments, alone with
    my sheep,

And still fear lest the terrible glory evanish like sleep!

For I wake in the gray dewy covert, while Hebron
    upheaves

The dawn struggling with night on his shoulder, and
    Kidron retrieves

Slow the damage of yesterday's sunshine.

xv.

                                I say then,— my song

While I sang thus, assuring the monarch, and ever
    more strong

Made a proffer of good to console him — he slowly
    resumed

His old motions and habitudes kingly. The right
    hand replumed

His black locks to their wonted composure, adjusted
    the swathes

Of his turban, and see — the huge sweat that his
    countenance bathes,

He wipes off with the robe ; and he girds now his
    loins as of yore,

And feels slow for the armlets of price, with the
    clasp set before.

He is Saul, ye remember in glory,— ere error had
    bent

The broad brow from the daily communion ; and
    still, though much spent

Be the life and the bearing that front you, the same,
    God did choose,

To receive what a man may waste, desecrate, never
    quite lose.

So sank he along by the tent-prop, till, stayed by
    the pile

Of his armor and war-cloak and garments, he leaned
  there awhile,

And so sat out my singing,— one arm round the
  tent-prop, to raise

His bent head, and the other hung slack — till I
  touched on the praise

I foresaw from all men in all times, to the man
  patient there,

And thus ended, the harp falling forward.   Then
  first I was 'ware

That he sat, as I say, with my head just above his
  vast knees

Which were thrust out on each side around me, like
  oak-roots which please

To encircle a lamb when it slumbers.   I looked up
  to know

If the best I could do had brought solace: he spoke
  nòt, but slow

Lifted up the hand slack at his side, till he laid it
  with care

Soft and grave, but in mild settled will, on my brow :
  thro' my hair

The large fingers were pushed, and he bent back
　　my head, with kind power —

All my face back, intent to peruse it, as men do a
　　flower,

Thus held he me there with his great eyes　that
　　scrutinized mine —

And oh, all my heart how it loved him ! but where
　　was the sign ?

I yearned — "Could I help thee, my father, invent-
　　ing a bliss,

I would add to that life of the past, both the future
　　and this.

I would give thee new life altogether, as good, ages
　　hence,

As this moment, — had love but the warrant, love's
　　heart to dispense ! "

XVI.

Then the truth came upon me.　No harp more — no
　　song more ! outbroke —

XVII.

" I have gone the whole round of Creation : I　saw
　　and I spoke !

I, a work of God's hand for that purpose, received
    in my brain

And pronounced on the rest of his handwork —
    returned him again

His creation's approval or censure: I spoke as I saw.

I report, as a man may of God's work — all's love,
    yet all's law !

Now I lay down the judgeship he lent me. Each
    faculty tasked

To perceive him, has gained an abyss, where a dew-
    drop was asked.

Have I knowledge ? confounded it shrivels at wis-
    dom laid bare.

Have I forethought ? how purblind, how blank, to
    the Infinite care !

Do I task any faculty highest, to image success ?

I but open my eyes,— and perfection, no more and
    no less,

In the kind I imagined, full-fronts me, and God is
    seen God

In the star, in the stone, in the flesh, in the soul and
    the clod.

And thus looking within and around me, I ever
    renew

(With that stoop of the soul which in bending
    upraises it too)

The submission of Man's nothing-perfect to God's
    All-Complete,

As by each new obeisance in spirit, I climb to his
    feet !

Yet with all this abounding experience, this Deity
    known,

I shall dare to discover some province, some gift of
    my own.

There's one faculty pleasant to exercise, hard to
    hoodwink,

I am fain to keep still in abeyance, (I laugh as I
    think)

Lest, insisting to claim and parade in it, wot ye, I
    worst

E'en the Giver in one gift.— Behold ! I could love
    if I durst !

But I sink the pretension as fearing a man may
    o'ertake

God's own speed in the one way of love : I abstain,
    for love's sake !
— What, my soul ? see thus far and no farther ?
    when doors great and small,
Nine-and-ninety flew ope at our touch, should the
    hundredth appall ?
In the least things, have faith, yet distrust in the
    greatest of all ?
Do I find love so full in my nature, God's ultimate
    gift,
That I doubt his own love can compete with it ?
    here, the parts shift ?
Here, the creature surpass the Creator, the end,
    what Began ? —
Would I fain in my impotent yearning do all for
    this man,
And dare doubt He alone shall not help him, who
    yet alone can ?
Would it ever have entered my mind, the bare will,
    much less power,
To bestow on this Saul what I sang of, the marvel-
    lous dower

Of the life he was gifted and filled with ? to make
such a soul,

Such a body, and then such an earth for insphering
the whole ?

And doth it not enter my mind (as my warm tears
attest)

These good things being given, to go on, and give
one more, the best ?

Ay, to save and redeem and restore him, maintain
at the height

This perfection,—succeed with life's dayspring,
death's minute of night ?

Interpose at the difficult minute, snatch Saul, the
mistake,

Saul, the failure, the ruin he seems now,—and bid
him awake

From the dream, the probation, the prelude, to find
himself set

Clear and safe in new light and new life,—a new
harmony yet

To be run, and continued, and ended — who knows ?
— or endure !

The man taught enough of life's dream, of the rest
to make sure.

By the pain-throb, triumphantly winning intensified
bliss,

And the next world's reward and repose, by the
struggle in this.

XVIII.

" I believe it ! 'tis Thou, God, that givest, 'tis I who
receive:

In the first is the last, in thy will is my power to
believe.

All's one gift: thou canst grant it moreover, as
prompt to my prayer

As I breathe out this breath, as I open these arms to
the air.

From thy will, stream the worlds, life and nature,
thy dread Sabaoth :

I will ? — the mere atoms despise me ! and why am
I loth

To look that, even that in the face too ? why is it I
dare

Think but lightly of such impuissance? what stops
    my despair?

This ;— 'tis not what man Does which exalts him,
    but what man Would do!

See the king — I would help him but cannot, the
    wishes fall through.

Could I wrestle to raise him from sorrow, grow poor
    to enrich,

To fill up his life, starve my own out, I would —
    knowing which,

I know that my service is perfect.— Oh, speak
    through me now!

Would I suffer for him that I love? So wilt Thou
    — so wilt Thou!

So shall crown thee the topmost, ineffablest, utter-
    most Crown —

And thy love fill infinitude wholly, nor leave up nor
    down

One spot for the creature to stand in! It is by no
    breath,

Turn of eye, wave of hand, that Salvation joins
    issue with death!

As thy Love is discovered almighty, almighty be
    proved

Thy power, that exists with and for it, of Being
    beloved !

He who did most, shall bear most ; the strongest
    shall stand the most weak.

'Tis the weakness in strength that I cry for ! my
    flesh, that I seek

In the Godhead ! I seek and I find it. O Saul, it
    shall be

A Face like my face that receives thee : a Man like
    to me,

Thou shalt love and be loved by, forever ! a Hand
    like this hand

Shall throw open the gates of new life to thee ! See
    the Christ stand ! "

XIX.

I know not too well how I found my way home in
    the night.

There were witnesses, cohorts about me, to left and
    to right,

Angels, powers, the unuttered, unseen, the alive —
the aware —

I repressed, I got through them as hardly, as strug-
glingly there,

As a runner beset by the populace famished for
news —

Life or death. The whole earth was awakened,
hell loosed with her crews ;

And the stars of night beat with emotion, and
tingled and shot

Out in fire the strong pain of pent knowledge : but
I fainted not.

For the Hand still impelled me at once and sup-
ported — suppressed

All the tumult, and quenched it with quiet, and
holy behest,

Till the rapture was shut in itself, and the earth
sank to rest.

Anon at the dawn, all that trouble had withered
from earth —

Not so much, but I saw it die out in the day's tender birth ;

In the gathered intensity brought to the gray of the
    hills ;

In the shuddering forests' new awe ; in the sudden
    wind-thrills ;

In the startled wild beasts that bore off, each with
    eye sidling still

Tho' averted, in wonder and dread ; and the birds
    stiff and chill

That rose heavily, as I approached them. made
    stupid with awe.

E'en the serpent that slid away silent,— he felt the
    new Law.

The same stared in the white humid faces upturned
    by the flowers ;

The same worked in the heart of the cedar. and
    moved the vine-bowers.

And the little brooks witnessing murmured. per-
    sistent and low,

With their obstinate, all but hushed voices — E'en
    so ! it is so.

PROSPICE.

Fear death ? — to feel the fog in my throat,
    The mist in my face,
When the snows begin, and the blasts denote
    I am nearing the place,
The power of the night, the press of the storm,
    The post of the foe :
Where he stands, the Arch Fear in a visible form,
    Yet the strong man must go.
For the journey is done and the summit attained,
    And the barriers fall,
Though a battle's to fight ere the guerdon be
      gained,
    The reward of it all.
I was ever a fighter, so — one fight more,
    The best and the last!
I should hate that death bandaged my eyes, and
      forbore,
    And bade me creep past.

No! let me taste the whole of it, fare like my
    peers
    The heroes of old,
Bear the brunt, in a minute pay glad life's arrears
    Of pain, darkness, and cold.
For sudden the worst turns the best to the brave,
    The black minute's at end.
And the elements' rage, the fiend-voices that
    rave,
    Shall dwindle, shall blend,
Shall change, shall become first a peace, then a
    joy,
    Then a light, then thy breast,
O thou soul of my soul! I shall clasp thee again,
    And with God be the rest!